F
James, Melissa.
Long-lost father

LONG-LOST
FATHER

LONG-LOST FATHER

BY

MELISSA JAMES

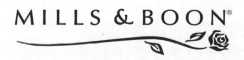

MILLS & BOON®

All Rights Reserved including the right of reproduction
in whole or in part in any form. This edition is published
by arrangement with Harlequin Enterprises II B.V. The
text of this publication or any part thereof may not be
reproduced or transmitted in any form or by any means,
electronic or mechanical, including photocopying,
recording, storage in an information retrieval system,
or otherwise, without the written permission of
the publisher.

MILLS & BOON and
MILLS & BOON with the Rose Device
are registered trademarks of the publisher.

First published in Great Britain 2006
Large Print edition 2007
Harlequin Mills & Boon Limited,
Eton House, 18-24 Paradise Road,
Richmond, Surrey TW9 1SR

© Lisa Chaplin 2006

ISBN-13: 978 0 263 19430 2
ISBN-10:   0 263 19430 2

Set in Times Roman 16¼ on 18½ pt.
16-0207-55806

Printed and bound in Great Britain
by Antony Rowe Ltd, Chippenham, Wiltshire

This book is dedicated to Lily Maya, for singing, dancing and demanding all the happiness that life can offer. To Chris, Chrisanya, Zeb and the family, for all you did to save a baby in a hospital in Kathmandu, who would never have lived without you.
Special thanks to the Institute for Deaf and Blind Children in Sydney, for helping me to understand the special needs of my brother's family, and for permission to use their marvellous facilities as a part of Casey's life.
Final thanks go to Mia Zachary, Olga Mitsialos and Rachel Robinson, for all their excellent suggestions. And to Maryanne and Diane. You know why.

CHAPTER ONE

"SO SHE MARRIED the prince and lived happily ever after in his beautiful castle." Samantha Holloway's fingers left the page to trail over her daughter's sleep-flushed cheek. "It's time for sleep now, princess."

The child's tiny Cupid's-bow mouth stretched wide in a yawn. "Oh, all right." The golden-brown eyes—so like her father's—turned to Samantha, soft and unfocused. Eyes as heartbreaking as they were beautiful, for while they were filled with expression, they were not filled with light. "D'you still love me lots and lots?"

Sam felt her throat close up as she caressed the feathery gold curls. "More than anything in the world, princess." To love and protect her darling girl was her life's mission.

Casey smiled, lighting twitching dimples, with a look of mischief that was her father's inheritance. Sam ached anew, seeing it. "Night-night, Mummy." After her prayer, she rolled over and pulled up her sheet before drifting off to sleep.

Sam returned the stuffed animals and discarded book back to their slots—and then she did the same for the rest of the house. Cleanliness wasn't a luxury or an obsession in Sam's home. It was a necessity she couldn't afford to neglect. A dropped toy was a potential hazard; spilled milk not immediately wiped dry could be worth crying over.

When your child was blind, mess was deadly.

When her work was done, Sam heaved a sigh of relief and wandered to her bedroom. She crossed to the window and looked out at the night through her neighbour's trees, luxuriating in the simple joy of silence and peace.

It was her time now…her time to live.

But I have no one to live it with.

Stop it! Self-pity is as destructive to you as it is to Casey.

She'd go relax on her hammock on the veranda. That was it. Let's get positive…

The light cotton dress slithered down steam-heated skin, pooling to a huddled heap around her feet. Her cream-coloured lacy underwear—her concession to femininity—followed piece by piece, dropped carelessly for the simple abandon of it. Then years of routine kicked in, and she laid them on the bed. She stretched, her hands sliding upward to lift her mop of fair curls through her fingers as she drank in the dark, still night. Shrugging off the responsible woman she must be during the day, even if it was only for an hour. As much as she loved Casey—and no woman could love her child more—she reveled in the glorious freedom of *quiet,* the peace of being alone. For now, she belonged only to the sweet, velvety summer night.

February nights in Sydney were steamy, heavy with the promise of storm, turning the lightest of clothing into unbearable fetters. She loved padding around the darkened house in as little clothing as possible, feeling the whispering breezes through her windows surrounding her. With a long, cool drink and her lightest sarong, lying on the hammock she could only set up on her veranda at night—lest Casey walk into it and hurt herself—and she could indulge her senses, lose herself in the pulsing silence of darkness.

Shimmering waves still rose from the ground as the earth cooled itself from the scorching heat of day. Her body took on its heat and pulse, the *waiting* for the storm, the pressure building, heat sliding into her pores. She took an ice cube into her mouth, letting it melt, and the cold liquid slipping down her throat in cool relief.

The build-up toward the distant rumble of thunder set her nerves jangling; the promise of electricity lashed in tiny whip-flicks along every nerve ending.

The glistening water of the inground pool, lit by floor lights, whispered her name. It was her only indulgence, renting a house with a safe, solar-heated pool. She told herself Casey needed hydrotherapy, but deep down she knew it was for her. A swim was the only way she could release the pressure of the day.

A perfect night for a swim…moonlight and starlight and dark, roiling clouds, terrifying and beautiful—she wanted to slide into them, become part of the night.

Stop the memories…

She had little time before the storm hit. She was all Casey had; she couldn't risk her life, as she used to when it didn't matter—before Casey gave her life strength, meaning and *love*.

Twenty or thirty hard laps would dissipate the tension, bring her back to reality.

She wouldn't admit that it was thinking of *him* that she wanted to escape.

A minute later, dressed in her favourite sky-blue one-piece swimsuit, she plunged into the deep end, her splash coinciding with the distant crack of thunder from the clouds closing in on the Sydney Basin.

Tire yourself out and you'll stop thinking.

During the buildup to a storm, memories over-whelmed her. The tension took hold of her heart, body and soul, leaving her so *alone*, and the power of him came like a knight on a white charger to rescue her from endless isolation. Memories of his laughing face. Of him taking hold of her hand, something serious and intent inside those golden-brown eyes as her boss had introduced them at a swish poolside function at his fashionable Kew home.

"Samantha Holloway, this is my doctor, Brett Glennon. He saw you standing alone over here and wanted to meet you."

Brett had smiled at her as if he knew some-thing wonderful, amazing, that she didn't. World-weary at twenty-two, she'd waited for the trite line about Fate or something blatantly sleazy; but he'd looked at her kicked-off sandals, glanced down and said, "I never could resist a pair of bare feet as good-looking as that. My feet are jealous." And he'd kicked off his shoes, defying the disapproving looks of the formally clad guests with a conspiratorial grin that had melted her heart.

He was like that from the first, making her feel special and keeping her laughing. Life wasn't serious or tragic with Brett; she wasn't the Ice Princess—she was Sam, a young woman enjoying life with a man who saw beneath her cold facade to the scared girl inside.

Brett was the laughter she'd never known in her sterile world, the caring she'd always hungered for in the dark emptiness of the orphanage—and on their wedding night, he'd overcome her fears and introduced her to the passion she'd read about but never understood. For five exquisite months, he'd been the light in her starved life, the love, the reason to get up every day. Brett was *everything*.

And then he was gone, and the sun disappeared behind the clouds of her life: she was back to the mistrust and anger, the abandonment and dark emptiness, of life in the orphanage and repeated bouts of foster care…the *nothing*. He'd left her behind.

Yet for a little while, she had been loved—or at

least she'd believed so at the time. Sometimes she wished she could have remained that blissfully ignorant.

Still, he hadn't left her totally alone. He'd left her a priceless treasure. Every day she thanked God for the gift of her beautiful daughter. To Sam, Casey was perfect, precious—her beloved daughter, her only family. She'd spent six years on the run to keep them together. David and Margaret Glennon might be Casey's grandparents, but they'd only gain custody of her over Sam's dead body.

Don't think. Swim!

On a night like this it was impossible *not* to relive her time with Brett. He'd been gone for too long, and memories were all she had. But she ached with what she'd lost—the absolute love from a man who knew her inside and out.

Every so often the memories became overwhelming, so incredibly *real*. She could almost *feel* the tender brushing of his lips against her mouth, the gentle waft of cool breath, the whispered comments that made her choke with laughter, made her body come alive with need and her heart overflow with love at once; and tonight she was already aching, yearning for what could never be again…

Swim harder!

She turned at the end and struck out again. *Twenty. Twenty-one.*

The memories, beautiful and unforgettable, were worse than useless. Painful and bittersweet, they hurt her as much as his words after their first kiss. He'd caught her behind the palms surrounding the pool, laughing—and something in him had called to her, melting the frozen walls she'd built to keep all men at arm's length.

Her resolve had died by the end of that incredible kiss—and he hadn't been laughing when they'd finally parted. He'd said, his voice shaking and almost bitter, "Why couldn't I have met you three years from now?"

Don't think about it. Swim! You have only—

"Hello, Sam."

She gasped in water, halting midlap. Had she really *heard* that beautiful dark-malt-whiskey voice? *No! Don't drive yourself mad with hope!*

Yet she whimpered, "Brett." Hungering, craving...

"Yes, it's me." The dark, smooth voice was strong, sure—so masculine yet so cold. "Despite your best efforts to hide, I found you. I hear I have a daughter. I'd like to meet her."

She gasped again. Her eyes snapped open. She jerked backward in the water until she stood facing the shadows of the veranda from where the sound of his voice had come. No—it couldn't be Brett. He was…was—

Obviously *not* in an unmarked grave behind enemy lines in some war-forsaken tiny nation in Africa. All six feet of strong, dark-haired, golden male was right before her, *living, breathing*—and all she could do was gape at him while stinging tears rushed to her eyes.

"Brett?" The name was laden with disbelief, with terror, her whole body shaking: the rush of shock, from her fingertips to her reeling mind, seemed to have changed her very heartbeat, stopping and kick starting in painful waves. He was real…he was *real.*

"Hello, Sam." He stepped out of the languid darkness, into the soft brightness cast by the pool lights. Those eyes, those golden-brown laughing eyes, were dark with the intense emotion he was keeping under tight check.

Sam couldn't stop shivering; the world seemed to be spinning the wrong way. Her hand found the edge of the ladder, and she hung on for dear life. "Brett…" She sounded like the world's biggest idiot, repeating his name over and over, but she couldn't stop.

"Yes." His tone held no impatience; it held nothing at all.

"But…" The change from languid heat to ice-cold fear, from deepest fantasy to utter reality in a matter of seconds left her too disoriented to be coherent. "Africa…Mbuka…when did…?"

His face tightened. "If you mean when did I get back to Australia, almost two years ago." He lifted something in his hand—it was a walking stick. "I only got the all clear from my physiotherapist a week ago."

Two years. He'd been home two years, and she'd known nothing, thinking him dead.

It was too much. The sickness rushed to claim her. Her head drooped onto the ladder, but she breathed in water. Gasping, choking on one cough after another, she tightened her grip on the ladder as if it were a lifeline to sanity. Tears poured down her face.

She felt his warm, strong hands grasp under her arms. A moment later he'd lifted her out of the pool and hauled her against him, patting with a cupped hand against her upper back, pushing upward with the heel of his palm to clear the water. He kept working on her until the choking subsided. "That'll teach me to shock a woman in a pool," he murmured somewhere near her hair. "You'd think a doctor would know better."

Even the intimacy of his hand on her back, his voice so close, overwhelmed her. Six years of painful dreams, waking to emptiness, always alone but never letting anyone close…now he was here and…touching her… *Brett…*

There were times during the frantic days, the long, sleepless nights, when she thought she'd *die* for him to be here, to *touch* her one more time, to let her know she wasn't alone.

She choked again as the emotion came crashing down over her, and the more she tried to fight it, the bigger the burning ball of pain became, cutting off her breathing. The woman who'd never allowed herself the time or luxury to grieve for the husband she'd adored finally emerged from some dark place inside, demanding relief. Her legs shook too hard to support her. She dropped to her knees, buried her face in her hands and wept.

"Sam." He was so close she could smell the spicy aftershave he wore, the one she'd always loved so much. She'd bury her face into his throat and inhale it, inhale *him.* "I know this is a terrible shock. I had no choice but to do it like this, without warning."

Soft as the touch of butterfly wings, his fingertips touched her arms, caressing her. She felt the traitorous urge to snuggle against him, to take the comfort he was offering—

A bolt of panic sent her scuttling back. "D-don't touch me," she cried through the sobs still overwhelming her. She ached for his touch but hated that vulnerability after six years of strength and independence. She couldn't afford to be weak now.

You're at his feet in tears, a disgusted little voice said inside her. *Is that strong?*

"Okay." His voice grew deeper, hard yet rich with sensuality. "It's your choice. But could you adjust that thing you're almost wearing?"

Oh! The shock stilled her tears like a twisted-off tap. Gulping and hiccuping, she looked down and saw her old, favourite swimsuit had gone patchy in places, delicately see-through. She groped for her sarong and scrambled away from him, hitching it over her breasts. Unable to stop herself, her gaze lifted to his.

The tight-leashed control she'd sensed in him must have slipped just a little, for his dimples twitched. "You'd better get dressed now, Sam.

It's been a long time—for me, at least—and you're still the most beautiful woman I know."

She crossed her arms over her breasts in guilty confusion. The winds, cooling now, sent a chill down the length of her overheated body. She shuddered, but with a massive effort she managed to stop her teeth from chattering. "W-why are you here?"

His gaze remained steady on her face. "You're shivering on a night as hot as this—you're in shock. Dry off and get dressed or you'll end up sick."

She jumped unsteadily to her feet and fled into the house, locking her bedroom door. She leaned against it for a minute or more, just shaking, drawing deep breaths. She couldn't think, could only feel right now—and what she felt was sheer panic.

She reached out with trembling hands to gather up her forgotten towel and dried herself.

"Sam? Are you all right? You've been in there a long time."

Frantically she pulled herself together. "I'll be right there." She scrambled into her underwear and the plain cotton sundress she'd kicked under the bed and then used a second towel to fluff her hair semi dry. Time, she needed just a little more time to think…

On the other side of the door waited the husband she'd been told was dead.

She walked through to the living room and turned on the lights to negate the sensual, soft, deep velvet of night and the memories that were too strong, too beautiful, for either of them to forget, too dangerous to remember.

Brett waited for her by the open double glass doors leading to the small back veranda, arms folded, leaning on the doorpost.

It seemed some things didn't change. He still wore his favourite hip hugging jeans and a black Screaming Jets T-shirt. The evening shadow showed that he hadn't shaved since morning, giving him a rough, unfinished look that had always melted her.

He'd seemed a living oxymoron to her at first: a high-born doctor, the son of a judge, dressed like a rock star. Then, as she'd come to know him, she'd seen beneath to the boy forced to wear designer labels and always looking perfect for the world, as expected of a Glennon. But Carlton Brett Glennon, while loving his wealthy, socially active family and remaining close to them, had rebelled against his parents' perfect standards of dress and expectation from his teen years. From the day they'd met, he'd impressed her by caring more for his patients than his status, or the car he drove: the exact opposite of his socially conscious family he still somehow managed to love and respect—at least he had until he'd left for the tiny African nation of Mbuka to join Doctors for Africa, when their expectation had been for him to be a top Melbourne surgeon.

Did he want that, now, too? Would he finally fulfil his parents' hopes for him, and join the professional A-list?

She shook herself. Whatever he'd been when he'd loved her, things were different now. *I'm not the girl who ran from the threat of the Glennons. I will stand and fight this time!*

Then she noticed that he was pale beneath his tanned skin and he was shifting what was obviously his bad leg in an effort to find comfort. "Sit down, Brett," she said, aching for him, for his pain. "Put your leg up if it's hurting you."

The grin he directed her way was strained. "Watch it, I might think you care. All those tears and concern about my leg." He limped to the chaise lounge she'd found at a garage sale and lowered himself onto it with a sigh of relief. His cane clattered to the wooden floor.

And the spell broke. Brett was achingly familiar yet so distant, a man she'd once loved with all her starved heart. Now he was a stranger, and the memories of all they had shared only added to the awkwardness of this meeting. What were they now?

We are Casey's parents and have shared memories. That's all there can be.

"Don't play games, Brett." She knew her voice was curt, but she couldn't help it. He *looked* so much like the man she'd fallen so hopelessly in love with. The Brett who had brought her to life, the man who'd taught her how to live, to laugh and love.

She had to bury those memories. Brett was Casey's father, but he was also a Glennon: a man whom she had no doubt was still close to his parents, since he had always been before.

And his parents were the people who'd threatened to prove her an unfit mother, and take Casey from her by force.

David and Margaret Glennon, secure in family love and with wealth to back them up, didn't care if they left her all alone, as she'd been before; all they knew was that Casey was a Glennon, and deserved better than the penniless orphan mother who had nothing but love to give her. They'd wanted her to give Casey life and then leave as if she'd never existed.

What if that was why Brett had found her? Had he come to take Casey from her?

CHAPTER TWO

SHE WAS SLAMMING the emotional shutters down on him.

Brett thought he'd steeled himself for this—after all, he'd seen it all before, but he thought he'd helped her past all the insecurity and pain in her childhood of neglect had branded on her heart. But she'd seemed terrified by his appearance, and while he'd half expected that—he must have seemed like a ghost—he still hadn't seen a sign of happiness that he was alive.

The one thing that had kept him going until now was the hope she'd be thrilled he wasn't dead. That she might run into his arms to rejoice at his resurrection…but she'd *shrunk* from his touch.

Did that mean she'd prefer him to be dead? Why? *Why?*

"I'm not playing games," he replied, his voice curt with the pain he'd had to bury deep inside for too long. "*I'm* the one who never got any letters from you once I finally notified my family that I was alive. *I'm* the one who missed the calls that never came. *I'm* the one who's been looking for you for almost two years." He dragged in a breath. "I had to find out I was a father through my parents—but I discovered I had a *daughter* through a private detective. I had to learn her name through a *stranger* I paid to find you."

She flushed and turned away, her hands fiddling in the deep pockets of her blue sundress. Her hair was the same, the silver-blonde curls worn loose; she was barefoot, like the hippie he used to tease her about being. He'd loved her that way—the barefoot angel, his sweet nonconformist. She'd kicked her sandals off at the party where they'd met—that had drawn him to her. In a place full of stuffed shirts trying to impress each other, she'd been a lovely phantom of freedom.

It seemed they still had that in common—no need to impress anyone or to *be* anyone but themselves. But what else did they have? Did he even know her anymore?

"You could have left a forwarding address, Sam," he said, forcing calmness into his voice, willing his heart to the same. Anger and accusation would get them nowhere. "Were you so relieved that I was dead you just left me behind?"

"You know nothing about what I went through," she said, her voice barely audible through its shaking. "Maybe you can understand that in my grief for a husband I barely knew, I decided that starting over was best." She lifted her brows as she finished the words, trying for a sarcasm that didn't come off. Sam had never been any good at sarcasm, he thought with an unwanted shaft of tenderness.

But my Sam was never a coward, either.

"By changing your name and leaving no for-warding address?" he repeated the point, as cool as he could manage. "You never thought of checking with my parents or Doctors for Africa, to see if I could be alive? My parents were frantic about you and their grandchild. You never considered they'd need her when they lost me—or that she'd love to know the only extended family she has?"

Her nostrils flared; her lips were white with strain. "I don't have enough experience with loving families to have thought of that. Sorry." She didn't sound bitter, just resigned...yet some-thing simmered beneath the surface, some extreme emotion she wasn't willing to show him.

Once, Sam had shared her every thought, her every insecurity and bad memory with him.

You've been apart six years, his inner voice jeered. *What did you expect—that while your life blew apart, time stood still for her?*

He sighed. "I'd have thought your background was even more reason. You finally had a family, didn't you? My parents welcomed you into the family—"

"Despite the fact that I was a nameless orphan," she agreed softly, "and not worthy of the honour of gaining the affections of a Glennon."

What the hell did *that* mean? "I never once thought of you that way."

"I know," she said, still expressionless. What was she hiding?

"My parents were good to you," he growled, testing that particular water.

Something fleeting crossed her face, then disappeared—an emotion as heartfelt as it was private. "They were very good to me." Her voice held no inflection whatever.

Oh, man. A far greater distance separated them than a mere twelve feet of space. He felt like a soldier invading a fortress on his own, ramming his head against invisible barricades.

So much for those years of dreams in Mbuka, envisioning the joy of their reunion. Those dreams had gotten him through a life so dark and vile, so *alone,* that he could barely stand to think about what it had taken just to survive. He'd focused on coming home to Sam. She was his hope, his joy, the future, the only reason to want to get out of bed each day. A day filled with patching up people with little chance of surviving another week; a day where he was a prisoner of war and his medical skills were all that kept him alive, doctoring people who held life so cheap they'd shoot their mothers for food...

In the compounds and ragged camps, deserts and dank jungles of Mbuka's changing war zones, clinging to this moment had been his only hope.

Coming home hadn't done a damn thing to stop the nightmares, the shaking, the times when he'd just zone out and not know where he was, lost in memories an Olympic sprinter couldn't outrun. During two years of grueling physical therapy after the reconstruction of his knee, and repeated bouts of infection, he'd snatched the dying vestiges of his dream and hung on to them with a mindless tenacity that defied reason. He'd shut out the demons of doubt that whispered to him.

She'd never been there for your calls from Africa...and her calls late at night had been strained, scaring the hell out of you. Remember?

But he'd blanked it out. Sam hadn't left *him*; they'd been so happy! Surely when he found her, he'd find home at long last...because home was in Sam's arms, in the heart he'd always known had been totally his.

Well, he'd found her again, and he'd seen how she felt about it. While he'd used every resource of strength he'd had not to haul her against him and lose his living nightmare in her loving kiss, inside her welcoming arms and body, all she'd done was scramble to put distance between them.

A distance as emotional as it was physical. A distance she seemed determined to keep there.

So his parents were right: she'd escaped from *him;* she'd been glad he was dead. She'd found a new life in Sydney, leaving a trail so faint that it took almost two years to get a handle on her whereabouts.

Was the memory of what they'd been to each other so insignificant in her eyes? Was *he* so unimportant to her?

The child was definitely his; he'd seen the pictures of their child, a girl named Casey. The eyes were his, as were the dimples. There was no way Sam could claim her daughter was another man's. He'd get DNA tests if he had to.

But, damn it, he shouldn't have to—not with Sam, *his* Sam, whom he'd once trusted with his life, his heart and his entire future. Never in his vilest dreams had he believed that Sam could be this hard, so selfish as to disappear without trace, to take his child away from his parents, to deny them the comfort of his only child when they believed he was dead.

"What happened?" she broke into his reverie, sounding as if she was driven to ask. "To your leg, I mean."

Funny that he'd been the one so long in a war zone, facing life and death every day, fighting death more than once; yet the real question wasn't about him. *What happened, Sam? What changed you?*

He shrugged, feeling the shadows fall down on him. If he was going to break through Sam's barriers, he had to lower some of his own. But the memories of Mbuka—oh, God help him, would he ever forget? Just getting through each night without taking something to kill the dreams— dreams of what he'd lived through left him a shaking mass of pain, waking from fevered dreams drenched in sweat, screaming Sam's name like a prayer—seemed a victory.

"Brett?" Her voice sounded tentative, and he knew she'd seen him shaking.

"Sniper shot." If he didn't keep details to the bare minimum, the dreams would be worse tonight. "A splinter tribe near the Congo needed a doctor. But this time the cruciate ligament shredded into strips, stabbed the cartilage and got infected. I was no use to the warlords sick, so they left me out on the road to die. I was picked up by a tribe on the run with some compassion. They dosed me up with traditional healing cures and left me with some UN volunteers, who got me to a camp hospital."

"This time?" she whispered, her eyes filled with horror. "Is that what happened to you when you…disappeared."

He nodded; she deserved to know that much, to know why he hadn't phoned or come home to her. "It's an occupational hazard of being a doctor working in war zones. It took two years to escape from the first warlord, but I was captured again on the road south."

"Why didn't it hit the news?" she whispered, those amazing blue eyes of hers enormous with disbelief. "Your father has power and influence. Why didn't your disappearance hit the world media? Why didn't they look for you?"

"I signed the contract with my eyes open, knowing I could be shot or taken. It wasn't anyone's fault." He shrugged. "Everyone assumed I was dead." Funny, he knew that should mean that it wasn't Sam's fault, either, and he couldn't blame her for believing he was dead— but he *did* blame her. She'd loved him, damn it. Why hadn't she believed, as Mum and Dad had? Why had she just packed up and left?

"They didn't check to see if you were there? How fair is that on families?" she cried.

"They had the living to save. The boundaries change in war zones every day, Sam. There *is* no way to check, to be sure." He gave her a tired smile. "I'm sure they gave you the standard patter. 'There is a very slim chance he could be alive, but please get on with your lives. You may never know.'"

She gulped, bit her lip and nodded. Her eyes were dark with emotion. "I—I believed them. I had to get out. Your parents were so—so…"

He nodded. "If Dad could have gone there and throttled someone, he would. But he's in a wheelchair. He had a series of strokes." He looked at her. "He had the first a week after you left."

Her lashes fluttered down; she bit her lip. "I'm sorry, Brett. I didn't know."

"If you'd stayed, you *would* have known, Sam. Would it have changed anything for you?" he asked, unable to hide the fury. "Would you have stayed to help them through the nightmare? Would you have given the gift of their grandchild, my only child, to my sick parents? Maybe you wouldn't have turned into a human shadow, changing your name and hiding my daughter from my family—her family, who only wanted to know and love her?"

She stood still, unmoving, her pallor even more strongly marked. She either couldn't or wouldn't answer him.

He watched and waited. From experience he knew Sam would rush into speech and say whatever was on her mind if he kept his peace. He'd always learned a lot about her that way— but then, that had been when she'd loved and trusted him. Back when he'd held her in his arms as he'd waited for her to purge her pain. But in the lengthening silence, he knew how far he'd have to go to regain her trust.

That goes both ways, Sam, he thought grimly. Like it or not, they had to deal with each other. If she thought he'd walk out on his daughter, she'd better think again.

It seemed they both had some thinking to do. The one thing he'd banked on in this living nightmare was that Sam would be the girl he'd fallen in love with, loved so hard and deep that he'd married her after only eight weeks. But she *had* changed, so profoundly he found it difficult to recognize her. At this moment he didn't know if the Sam he'd loved and would have trusted with his life still existed inside the lovely yet withdrawn woman in front of him.

"Coffee?" she asked when the quiet stretched out to unbearable proportions.

"If you have decaf." At this time of night caffeine kept his mind active and led to the kind of visions that made him reach for the tranquilisers.

"Okay." With relief in her eyes, she left—no doubt to gather her thoughts. Her legs and hands were shaking. She held on to pieces of furniture as she walked.

She was still in shock. As a doctor, he knew he needed to go easy on her and wait before he made any judgments. Anything else was unfair to Sam.

To his surprise, he found he needed time, as well. He thought he'd known exactly what he was going to say to her, but his mind had emptied the moment he'd seen her in the pool, as lithe and beautiful as he remembered.

He sighed and rubbed his knee; it was aching badly. He'd have to take a painkiller soon, but he wanted to be coherent for what was coming.

He'd never felt so lost or alone in his life, as if he was still missing in action...

Or maybe it was his world that had gone missing. His tunnel-vision focus for so many years had been getting home to Sam, his light and life. But that particular tunnel had been blasted out of existence, as if he'd stepped on an emotional land mine. He didn't know what to do or say to get his life back, the only life he'd ever wanted apart from spending a few years serving his fellow man in Africa. He'd had it all planned...living in his beloved Melbourne, a heart surgeon, with Sam by his side. Starting a family when they returned to Australia, satisfied they'd done their part for humanity.

It seemed that everything he'd ever dreamed of had been relegated to the past. His shattered knee would heal eventually, and the moment it did, he'd accept the surgical residency he'd been offered in Melbourne's top hospital. But his African dream had exploded in his face within weeks. He already had a child, but she was a stranger to him. And he didn't know his wife anymore. *His* Sam lived for him, made his life hers; *his* Sam would have moved heaven and earth to reach Africa and find him.

This Sam watched him like a hawk, didn't rush into his arms, didn't cry joyful tears to know he was alive. This Sam didn't *need* him, and he didn't have a clue where to go from here.

Give her time…give yourself some, too. Trouble was, he felt he'd been marking time for years. He might *need* time, but he couldn't convince his heart and body of that need—others were crowding it out with their long-denied demands.

"Here." A soft voice, a gentle touch, and he looked up to see her standing above him, holding a steaming cup. Her face held question…and just for a moment, her luminous eyes, the colour of a spring sky, were touched with caring. She smelled fresh and clean, like the pool. Her voice was still sweet, almost singsong; she finished every sentence with a tiny lilt, as though she was asking an unconscious question.

So some things hadn't changed. He shook himself and smiled at her. "Thanks, Sam." Testing the boundaries, he let his fingers brush hers as he took the cup from her.

Her eyes darkened; her lids fluttered down, tender and languorous. Her lips parted—then she bit the lower one and came back to reality. "You're welcome. You look tired," she added with a gruffness that covered the husky tone she always used when he touched her.

Does that mean she hasn't *gotten over me?*

She moved back to the lounge opposite his, her face shuttered again. She didn't know what he wanted and wasn't giving an inch until she knew.

Obviously it was time to cut to the chase. "I'd like to meet my daughter."

She gripped her hands together so tight he could see the bone through the knuckles…and for the first time noted how thin, how delicate she'd become. Her skin, once pale and translucent, now seemed transparent.

"She'll be thrilled to find out she has a father. Most of her friends have families. She started asking about you a few months ago." Her hesitation was palpable. "Brett, you need to know something about Casey—"

"That she's blind?" he asked bluntly. "That's why you aren't working as a secretary anymore. It's why you only work on reception two days a week at the Deaf and Blind Children's Centre. So you can take her. You can stay with her."

Sam ran her tongue over her top lip before she nodded. "She's not at school full-time until the end of summer. I need to work, but I want to be with her as much as possible."

"How strong is her disability? What percentage of sight does she have?" The question had been in his mind since the detective had first told him. "Is she legally or profoundly blind? Is there any chance of optic regeneration through surgical procedure?"

Sam's eyes flashed. "This isn't a preliminary examination, Dr. Glennon. You're not her doctor, you're her father."

Stung, he retorted, "Pardon me, but since my daughter is five and I've never met her, it's hard for me to be emotional about this. I didn't see her birth or change her nappy, do a night feed or hold her when she cried." He shrugged. "Maybe I'd have been more emotional if I'd known her the past two years. She and I could have shared a lot—like our physical therapy classes."

Like a balloon pricked, the fight went out of Sam. "You're right." Her eyes closed over tears; she looked lost, defeated…and he remembered the reports from the detective. If he'd gone through hell in Mbuka and during recuperation, her life hadn't been anyone's picnic. Yet she'd not only survived, she'd adapted, changed her life for their child's sake and made a success of it.

He sighed, rubbing his brow. "I'm having a hard time with this. I thought you'd at least be glad that I'm alive."

"I am. I am!" she cried, looking wretched. "But I feel like a mouse that can't get off one of those treadmills. I didn't expect this. I had no notice you were coming—"

"Would you still be here if I'd given you notice?" he asked with all the force of the cynicism he felt welling inside.

She drew in a quick breath. "I don't know," she admitted with all the frankness he'd once loved in her. "I don't know why you're here. What do you want from me, Brett?"

Everything. But he'd be an idiot to say it now; he wasn't even sure if it was true. What he'd planned for and dreamed of for so many years had been coming home to *his* Sam. But while this woman looked like his Sam, sounded like her, she sure as hell didn't act like her. He wanted *his* wife, the life and family he'd dreamed of sharing with her.

So he chose the easy option. "I want to see my daughter, Sam. I want to spend time with her, to go places with her—"

But stark terror flashed through her eyes. "You can't take her anywhere without me. She—she doesn't know you. She doesn't take well to strangers. You have to see her with me here."

He frowned, feeling the emotional undercurrents pulling him into unknown waters. "For now, I just want to meet her, Sam."

"So long as you know," she muttered.

"That's fine—for now," he said, refusing to pull his punches. "But Casey has a family she's never met. I want to take her to Melbourne and let my parents and sister spend time with her. My parents are really anxious to meet her. She has cousins, too—"

"No!"

The gritted snarl jolted him.

Brett stared at her white face, her burning eyes, and knew that whatever Sam's problem was, they were near the heart of it. "You can't deny Casey's right to a relationship with her family. *You* know how badly that could affect the rest of her life."

Sam strode over to him, her face almost completely white and her eyes almost black with an emotion he hadn't been able to define until now. It was panic—blind panic. "You're not taking her from me, Brett."

It was obvious that by her intense reaction to his request, something was missing in this scenario. "I never said I wanted to take her *from* you, Sam. I only want her to meet her family. Is that such an unreasonable thing to ask?"

"M-maybe not," she said, her voice throbbing with hidden fear. "But you can't take her anywhere without me. Where she goes, I go."

Wishing he could shake the confusion right out of his head, he frowned at her. "Why are you talking about this? I haven't even met Casey."

Sam, so pale moments before, flushed again, soft and rosy. With her curls drying around her face, she looked so much—so *damn* much—like the angelic Sam he'd fallen in love with all those years ago, he ached.

"I know," she muttered, looking at her feet. "But if your parents want grandchildren to fuss over, you can find another woman easily and have the sort of family, the sort of children your family will—" She skidded to a halt, looking confused and guilty.

Not half as confused as he felt just by looking at her. She was blurting out what was on her mind now, as he'd planned; but none of it made sense to him. He was lost in looking at her. She was so sweet, so pretty in her confusion, he ached. Ached to turn back the clock and change choices that had been set in stone before he'd met her. Ached to haul her close and tumble down the barriers she'd put up between them.

The thought of making love to her made him burn inside, so fierce and hot that he had to force his mind back to the real issue. He needed to be calm and focused. "Casey deserves to know who she is. This isn't about your past, Sam," he added gently, knowing how hard this would hit her. But someone had to tell her, and he was the only father Casey had.

Unless Sam has found another man and Casey has already accepted him as her father?

"This is about Casey and her needs," he went on, ignoring the dark coils of jealousy that sprang up at the thought of another man touching Sam. "Why isn't she the *sort* of child my family will welcome? I know they can be a bit snobbish about dress and appearance, but they've never stopped me doing what I want with my life. They're dying to meet Casey. They have a room full of presents for her, stuff recommended by the Royal Blind Society. They want to meet her so badly. She's their granddaughter, Sam, their flesh and blood."

After a moment, she sighed. He saw her hands trembling. "I didn't mean it like that," she muttered low. "It's not that..."

"Then what *is* it? You said she'd asked about me. Are you trying to keep me from her, Sam? Would you deprive her of her father, of her family heritage, so you won't be alone?"

At that he saw the faltering of that fierce lioness, saw her resistance stumble, leaving a crack of vulnerability shining through.

"If she finds out the truth one day—that she has a whole family in Melbourne that you've kept from her—she'll resent the hell out of you for keeping her from them. Casey deserves to experience the love of extended family that's every kid's right. You should understand that, Sam. Do you still lie awake at night wondering who you are, wondering where your mother is and why

she left you? Why your dad didn't hang around?"
He waited a moment, but she didn't reply. "I
know you do, Sam. Everyone wants to know who
they are. Are you going to deny that security to
Casey just so you won't be alone anymore?"

She looked up at that; her eyes flashed. "You
don't understand."

"Make me understand," he said quietly. Trying
to see how she'd react to his words.

Sam turned and walked to the window, looking
out at the trees bending in the wind. The storm,
which had hovered off-coast for a while, was
closing in fast—but it didn't compare to the tur-
bulence inside her heart. Within minutes of
Brett's return he'd left Sam feeling raw and
exposed—and now she felt more vulnerable with
each probing word he uttered. On a night when
emotional roller coaster didn't begin to cover the
way she felt, she couldn't speak.

The laughing, live-for-the-moment Brett she'd
adored had become quiet, dark and driven. What
had he been through in Mbuka? Instinctively she
knew whatever he'd told her so far had only
scraped the surface of his suffering. The almost
two years of therapy he'd endured showed how
close to death he'd come.

And now his father was ill, in a wheel-chair…and it was her fault.

Given what he'd been through, what his family had been through, she couldn't tell him about his father's threat to take Casey from her. Being an orphan who'd never had the priceless treasure of family, a heritage or any sense of belonging, she couldn't take those threats from Brett. She'd spent her entire life craving what he had. It wasn't his fault his family didn't find her good enough for their beloved son. How could she blame them for that, now she had Casey? She wanted the very best for her beautiful girl…

Brett might be the single greatest threat to her security in Casey's life and love at this moment, but he'd obviously suffered enough. For the sake of the love she'd once had for him—for Casey's sake, too; the Glennons were her grandparents—she must keep silent about the reason for her flight from Melbourne.

She may not know how it felt to belong or about being loved, but she knew about disillusionment and abandonment.

She lifted a shaking hand to wipe away the sweat she hadn't known was breaking out on her face until that moment. "There's nothing to understand. Casey and I are a double package, and that's all—and we both stay in Sydney."

She could see his gaze on her, searching her face; she forced her eyes to remain calm as she faced him down.

Eventually he sighed. "I'll play your game for now, but the playing field could shift sides without warning. I want to know my daughter."

"I wouldn't prevent you if I could." She'd take what advantage she could get, for as long as she could, but Brett was far too much a take-charge man to sit in the backseat for long. "You'll love her, I know you will. She's such a little imp at times, but so loving. You barely know she's blind half the time, she's so able and smart."

His eyes grew dark, shadowed again. "I'm sure I will love her—she's from both of us," he agreed. "As sure as I am that my family will love her just as she is. As sure as I am that having Casey to love would have helped my parents during the time they thought I was dead."

She'd expected a frontal attack, but at his words the world seemed to go elliptical, swaying around her in strange arcs. She reached out behind her to a chair, the closest thing she could find as an anchor. *I can't tell him, I can't!*

Silence seemed the only option. To vindicate herself at the cost of Brett's family, his stability and security, was too selfish.

As selfish as you've been all these years in keeping Casey from all the rights and privileges of being a Glennon?

The pain was too great to bear. Every way she looked, her choices, both past and present, hurt someone she cared about.

But all those other people at least have someone else to love. Casey is all I have.

"I'm sorry," she whispered, praying he would leave it at that, knowing he wouldn't.

He stared at her, frowning. "Even if you couldn't handle living with Mum and Dad, why didn't you at least stay in Melbourne? Then you'd have known I was alive the past two years." His voice came out raw and scraped with intense emotion. "You're my wife, Sam. I went through *hell* in Mbuka—but the real nightmare began when I came home and found out I could be a father to a child I'd never seen. I lay awake night after night, wondering if you were all right, if I had a son or daughter. Wondering why you'd run—and if you'd run from me." His lips pressed together and she knew he was in pain that was as much physical as it was emotional. "I *needed* you, Sam," he managed to get out through gritted teeth.

Her eyes closed as she prayed for strength. He was hitting her right in the heart with every word he spoke, because they came from *his* heart. "*You* needed *me?*" Her throat scratched on the words. "I was in hospital for weeks after you left, bleeding and in constant danger of miscarriage. I called you from the hospital, trying to talk as if nothing happened because I didn't want to upset you when you couldn't do anything about it! *I* needed *you,* Brett—"

"Is that where you were? When I called and my parents said you were out?" His voice was dark and strained. "And why you sounded so distracted when you called me."

She drew a deep breath and nodded. "We all agreed to act like normal. We didn't want to upset you when you had so many lives dependent on your skills and ability to concentrate. But I obviously failed. I'm sorry. It must have worried you."

The silence was broken by a pounding *boom* of deep thunder, the wildness of a summer storm in Sydney. Lightning hit moments later, just to the right of the house. The lights flickered off and on, and in the flash of light she saw the stillness of remembered pain on his face and the deep relief of a worst fear unrealised.

"There was no one else, Brett," she said quietly. "If I sounded strange, it was because I was alone and scared. I needed you with me, but you were off saving the world. I didn't blame you, but abandonment goes both ways. You left for Mbuka within two months of our wedding—"

His voice was full of stress. "You knew I'd signed the contract with Doctors for Africa before we met. I was locked into two years' service. The people at the refugee camp were relying on me for their lives. But if you wanted me home, all you had to do was tell me you were pregnant and bleeding. I'd have come home on the first flight."

"But you'd have resented me for forcing you to turn your back on your lifelong dream," she insisted wearily. "You were so passionate and eloquent about meeting the desperate need in Mbuka. Casey's existence, then her blindness, would have kept you here. There are few good facilities for a blind child in a war zone, Brett."

In the silence, a clock ticked…and the next rumble of thunder came.

"You didn't give me the chance—or a choice, Sam. You didn't tell me." Brett's voice was harsh.

"You talked so movingly about the plight of the refugees when we met. You said you understood why I had to go…you said you'd come soon. Do you *know* how hard it was just being there, day after day? I lost more people than I saved and saw the most horrific injuries I'll ever see, knowing they were inflicted by the guy in the next bed half the time. Desperate people poured in to the camp day and night. I worked around the clock without a break except to eat and snatch an hour's sleep." As if in agreement, lightning forked across the sky, almost right over the house. "Do you know how often I *ached* for my wife to be with me? If I'd have known why, I'd have felt less abandoned by the time I was kidnapped by the rebels."

By the time I was out of hospital, I was on the run from your parents and their threats to take Casey from me, to have me proven an unfit mother by any means they could. "You never mentioned to me how bad it was there when we talked," she said, giving him some sort of answer. "Would it have been a safe place for Casey to be born?"

"Maybe not—but you didn't know that, so that can't be the reason."

The first patter of rain on the roof was normally a sound she welcomed, but tonight she barely noticed. The bulldog in Brett hadn't changed; he grabbed on to what he wanted to know and hung on with a tenacity that outlasted every other objection—and got him his way in the end.

"The doctors said I couldn't stress myself in any way—I had to rest to keep Casey alive," she said, knowing this much she could say. "Handling your upset and fear, frantically trying to get home because I was sick—" She left it there, knowing she'd said enough. "And then—"

"Yes, we keep coming back to it, don't we?" His tone was grim, as dark as the eyes boring into hers. So sure he was right in his belief that she'd abandoned his family. Yes, he was the same old Brett. What he thought, wanted or believed had to be the best thing for everyone.

"And *then,* when it was time to tell you," she went on inexorably, "the official at Doctors for Africa told us you were dead." She forced the word out, dragging in a breath so harsh he could probably hear it over the sounds of the storm finally hitting above them. "They told us there was no room for hope. I— I had to get out. I couldn't take all the memories."

She gulped down the ball of burning pain in her throat.

She hadn't heard him move, didn't know he'd

moved until she felt his hand on hers. "You could have stayed with the family. You wouldn't have been alone then."

You have no idea how alone I would have been.

She sighed and rubbed her aching forehead, feeling as if she had taken a sudden fever. "I feel like I'm stuck on a whirligig, just with you being here. I had to accept your death, to put you behind me. I *had* to forget to stay sane."

"Did you manage it, Sam? Did you forget me?" His fingers moved up her wrist and arm, soft and slow, and she shuddered in longing. Oh, the heady delight, not just of sensuality but of *touch*. Not a child's wonderful hugs but the touch of a man who understood that she couldn't be perfect, couldn't always be strong...

"There's no point in sharing our memories. We both know the truth. I know you loved me. But you were my *life*. Your work was your true love, your passion. It was *important*. I always knew I came second."

His hand stilled on her arm. "Is that the reason why you didn't tell me about Casey?"

Half-shamed, she nodded. "I didn't know whether you'd come home to us. I didn't want to know if I was going to come second again."

He winced, his eyes haunted. "You could have given me the chance. You could have trusted me."

"I did…in your commitment, your belief that you were in the right place, doing the right thing for humanity. It was almost all you talked about while we were together. I was scared you'd tell me what the people of Mbuka were going through and they needed you more than I did."

Having said so much, she felt drained, shaking with emotion. She'd wanted, *needed* this for so long? But now he was here, dreams had intertwined with her most vivid nightmares, and she couldn't find a way to untangle them.

You were never good enough for my son. You know nothing about family life. What makes you think you could ever be a good mother? David Glennon's words haunted her. *Give my son back his life when he returns from Africa—and give us the child. We'll raise it as a Glennon deserves. You can't give any child what they need to be safe and happy.*

Maybe she hadn't been raised in a family, and she'd always known she wasn't good enough for Brett. But David Glennon had been wrong about one thing. She'd turned herself into a good mother by constant work and determination. She'd never give Casey to the Glennons!

But she didn't know yet what she was up against, and Brett's silence wasn't helping.

"What do you want, Brett?" she asked wearily. "It's obvious you want something from me, not just Casey. Are you waiting to tell me that you want a divor—?"

He'd turned her into his arms, his mouth covering hers, before the word was complete. The kiss was frantic, full of a hunger so strong it knocked her off her emotional perch. She moaned into his mouth, *alive* for the first time in so long, aching and *hungry*. She gave kiss for kiss, knowing she'd have to pay for this weakness later, but finally, *at last,* she was a woman again…

Brett held her hard against him. "Does it feel like I want a divorce?" he demanded against her mouth. "Does it feel like I've forgotten you or replaced you?"

She couldn't answer; she was shaking, not with fear, but with *need,* and he knew that as much as she did. Her sensuality was something she'd never been able to hide from him.

"This—" he kissed her again, deep, hot and hard "—is what kept me together through the years of torture and blackness. The hope of being near you. Touching you. Having you in my bed again."

Her eyes slowly closed, and for a moment she gave herself to the unbearable beauty of his words. Making love—having that touch that made her feel so complete, so *loved...*

She gulped down the pain of aching temptation. "It's not enough." Her voice was drenched with the frantic need she heard in his words, and she shivered in violent craving. She *couldn't...*

"It feels like enough." His voice was rough with sensuality. He brushed his mouth over hers again, his hand caressing her waist, and it was all she could do not to puddle in a melted heap at his feet. "It feels damn good. We were always magnificent together. You can't hide from what we have—or from me."

She squeezed her eyes shut, but the vivid memories took over. Touching skin, mouths fused, caressing, whispering words of love...

She had to snap out of this, to face reality if he wouldn't. "What we *have,* apart from mutual attraction, is shared memories—and a child. Circumstances forced us to change, to become different people." She kept her gaze focused on his, watching his eyes darken in denial. "I'm not that adoring girl who needed you to fill her life. My life with Casey is busy and fulfilling." *Liar,* a voice in her mind whispered. "I'm not your satellite now. I can't be your one-person support-and-cheer squad. I can't change my life—or more importantly Casey's life—to make yours work for you. My first priority is Casey, and it will stay that way."

Brett's gaze darkened, his eyes almost black. She could see the intensity of suffering he'd been through in the years they'd been apart shining through in more than his damaged knee. He wanted more than her body—he needed her presence to give him strength to heal or at least drive away the anguish that obviously still hadn't left after two years back home.

But her life had changed. All her strength, all her resources of giving and support, had to remain focused on meeting Casey's needs. How could she give him what she no longer had?

The knowledge lay like lead over her heart and soul. Just being Casey's mother took every scrap of strength she had every day. She had nothing to give him—

Except my heart. And how do I trust him to not take all I have, including my daughter, and leave for Melbourne on the first flight?

Melbourne was no longer home. It was where his parents waited with a court order to stop her from leaving again; where they'd use their influence to have her proven an unfit mother, simply because she wasn't a Glennon, and didn't have a family name or background to give them. Then they'd take Casey from her…the only worthwhile thing in her life.

She swallowed the ball of pain in her throat. "What we once had is gone. I'm sorry, but I can't give you what I don't have."

His hands landed on her shoulders, holding her with gentle strength—the inner strength of knowing who and what he was that she'd always loved about him. "I don't believe it. Either you're lying to me or to yourself. You want me as much as I want you."

"That isn't the point. It's been a long time for me—but it's not enough. The issue isn't how we feel about each other." Barely able to move, she pushed wayward strands of hair from her eyes. "What you or I want doesn't matter. This isn't about us. Casey is my first, last and every duty of care. You should understand that as a doctor, even if you don't feel like her father yet—"

Before she could finish her words, a sleepy little voice came from the other end of the room. "Are you my father?"

CHAPTER THREE

SHE SOUNDS LIKE SAM in miniature...

Lost in a haze of passion, of *need* for Sam's touch, Brett reacted with the instinct of a man who'd lived in a place where to move too slow could mean death. He slewed his gaze to the open door off the open-plan lounge, to where the lilting voice had asked the half-curious question.

And he saw a tiny, mussed angel in Winnie the Pooh pyjamas.

Feathery curls a touch brighter than Sam's fell in tumbled disarray around little shoulders. A face as fine and spiritual as a Botticelli cherub was turned to him. Tiny features, a replica of her mother's, in a pale heart-shaped face. A mouth of baby pink was unsmiling yet not angry.

This is my daughter.

A jolt of awareness filled him, a gentle awakening of some emotion he'd long buried beneath anger and denial. She was his daughter; he could see a pair of twitching dimples beside her mouth and the enormous golden-brown eyes gazing in his direction.

The photos he'd seen hadn't done her beauty any justice at all. He couldn't stop staring at this haunting, delicate, beautiful child.

My daughter.

"Hello?" Casey's voice trembled with sudden uncertainty. "Mummy?"

He wanted to hit himself for being so stupid. *Lesson number one in being a daddy to a special-needs child: always answer her when she talks to you.*

"I'm here, sweetheart." Sam's voice was full of love.

Brett put a hand on her arm, willing her to stay where she was. After a short, searching glance, Sam nodded but held her ground.

"Hello, Casey." Brett's heart was beating fast. What would she think of him? Would she like him? Or—

"Hello." A tentative smile flitted across her face, lifting dimples, before she repeated her initial question. "Are you my father?"

Her face held only a polite smile. Impassivity

in a five-year-old unnerved Brett. There was nothing in her face to read. She was curious as to whether he was her father, that was all.

"Yes, Casey," he said softly. "My name's Brett Glennon. I'm your father."

She nodded, slow and cautious, not moving toward him or moving away. He realised she was keeping her distance, almost as if she was afraid...

Afraid of *him?*

Keeping his features schooled, he absorbed the pain. Casey saw more than he would have thought with those imperfect eyes. Had she seen past his gentle facade to the anger in his heart that *his* child, his *daughter,* should have such a terrible burden to bear? Did she wonder if her daddy wouldn't like her because she was blind?

This was a fear his daughter should never have had to go through—

And she wouldn't if I hadn't left for Africa.

And like that, the truth pounced on him, like a lion long crouched nearby, waiting to attack. Maybe he'd known all along. But he'd concentrated so much on where *Sam* had been, he'd forgotten what she'd borne alone in the years he'd been gone. If she'd stayed with his parents, he'd have known Casey the past two years—but he'd still have three years of unintentional neglect to make up for.

Not for the first time, he felt the knife-pang of regret for leaving Sam behind in the first place, for charging ahead with a dream despite the cost to others, for cementing a love that happened in the wrong time and place. By living *his* dream, he'd left her alone with a hard pregnancy, a new state and a special-needs child, and his parents with the consequences of an assumed death and his father's strokes.

He'd been so damn-fool arrogant to think *he* had to save the world instead of keeping his own world together. Been so sure his choice was right, cocky and confident that everything would fall into place for everyone he loved.

It hadn't worked out for anyone. Not for the refugees he'd gone to help—he'd been kidnapped too soon to be of use. It hadn't worked for his parents—his father had been wheelchair-bound for years from the shock of losing his son and grandchild at once.

It didn't work out for Sam, either. Not even for me.

He'd thought he'd been the victim in this scenario. Events tonight had shown him that he hadn't been the only one to make sacrifices.

It seemed he had a lot to make up for.

"I came to meet you, Casey," he said, hoping to start bridging a gap that should never have existed…but it did, and he had to deal with the reality of that. "I would have come a long time ago, but—" after a glance at Sam, he went on "—but I was living far away and I didn't know where you and Mummy had gone."

"Okay," Casey said, accepting his words at face value. She stuck out her hand. "It's nice to meet you, Mr.—" She groped for the name she'd already forgotten.

"My name's Brett Glennon, Casey." He limped forward and took her hand. Sam had trained their child in good manners—but then, blind children learned through hearing and touch, scent and instinct. Touching was Casey's way of "seeing" him.

"I'm very glad to meet you," he added, smiling at her even though he knew she couldn't see it. Casey possessed her mother's ability to send that piercing shaft of joy through him with the most simple of words and acts.

"You're smiling," Casey said. "I can hear it in your voice."

"Yes, I am," he replied, taken aback. "I'm just

so happy to meet you, Casey—and to discover that I have such a beautiful daughter."

"My name's Holloway," Casey said gravely, releasing his hand. "At school, the other kids who got a daddy and a mummy all got the same name."

"*Have,* Casey," Sam put in, her voice restrained. "The kids *have* a daddy and *have* the same name."

"Yeah, that," Casey agreed, her smile growing. "So why's your name different?"

Brett grinned. So she'd also inherited his tendency to tease…and his bulldog tenacity to get answers.

Cautiously he gave her an edited version of the truth. "Like I said, I was far away. I was living in a place called Africa when you were born. I'm a doctor and I wanted to help people who were hungry and suffering." With a flickered look at a withdrawn Sam, he added, "I was working where it was hard to get to a phone. I wish I had known about you, Casey. I would have come home to look after you both."

He searched Casey's face, wondering if she'd noticed his avoidance of her real question, but she'd veiled her reaction. Another wall of anguish slammed into him. That any five-year-old child, let alone his daughter, should know how to hide her emotions, struck his soul with a chilling feeling of wrongness.

Casey asked slowly, "Can I look at you?"

Sam said, "She means she'd like to—"

"I know, Sam." With a difficulty so strong it was pitiful, he managed to bend his knee. Balancing with a hand on the chair, then the coffee table beside it, he lowered himself to the floor before the little girl. Again he took Casey's hand—such a fragile thing—and lifted it to his face. "Go for it, kid," he said in a gentle voice.

Casey's fingers explored his face, walking along his skin in delicate pulses and strokes. She felt his closed eyes, tested the shape of his less-than-classic nose, his strongly defined cheek-bones, the line of his brow. She learned the shape of his ears. Her fingers probed his mouth, feeling the indents of his dimples beside it.

Question number one answered: she wasn't legally blind but profoundly blind. Legally blind children could see through thick glasses, make out blurry images by peering close enough. Casey must have no sight at all. What accident of birth or fate had caused it? Had the stress of her mother's pregnancy all alone caused this?

Could he have prevented Casey's disability if he'd been home and seen the signs of trouble before her optic nerve had become irreparably damaged?

"You have dimples, like me," Casey commented, jerking him from his reverie.

"And we have the same colour eyes," he added, without mentioning the actual shade. *She wouldn't understand*, he thought, and the pang of wistfulness hit him harder than he believed it could. He'd thought he'd accepted this…

But that was before he'd met her, this lovely child with the woman's mind.

Casey nodded thoughtfully. "Do I look like you?"

"A little bit," he said, feeling a strong sense of pride. This tiny angel, so haunting and *almost* perfect, had sprung from his loins, his blood, his love for Sam. "You look more like your mummy, which means you're very pretty."

A tiny hand fell onto his chest—and a frown marred her translucent face. "Why are you sad?" she asked. Either she knew she was pretty or such things didn't bother her.

Does she know what "pretty" is? She's never seen one beautiful thing in her life…

And again that hurt far more than he'd thought it would.

Then her words penetrated and he blinked. "What?"

"You walked funny and have a stick to balance. You have a sore leg. And you have sad lines," Casey said softly, "here—" she touched his mouth "—and here," touching his forehead.

"I might be old," he replied to gain time, stunned by what she'd said and how she'd reached her conclusions—and by the fact that she was right every time.

Casey's mouth turned down. "Your hand hasn't got any wrinkly bits. Your voice isn't old." She moved back, severing the fragile connection they'd been making.

Lesson number two: don't underestimate her because she can't see.

"Why were you fighting with Mummy?"

The way she put it wasn't a question; she was stating a fact and demanding answers. No, Casey wasn't a child to underestimate.

Sam jumped in before he could answer the child. "Casey—" she ordered in a no-nonsense, go-to-bed tone.

Brett frowned, surprising himself by siding with Casey. "She deserves to know, Sam."

Sam glared at him. "She's only five! She doesn't need to—"

"She's part of us," he said, again surprising himself, and turned back to Casey. "I sort of startled Mummy. She wasn't expecting me to come here. She thought I was still far away."

"You were yelling at her," Casey pointed out. "Don't you like Mummy?"

He twisted around, looking at his wife with a serious, intent expression. "Yes, Casey, I like your mummy. I always have, from the moment I met her."

He could see the rosy outline of Sam's cheek as she turned away. But the denial implicit in her stiff back slammed into his gut—then he saw that she was shaking. This night, this reunion, was taking a higher toll on Sam than he'd believed it could.

And behind his wife's turned back, on the sideboard, he saw it. A series of framed photos: a picture of them on their first date, holding hands and smiling, taken by a roving photographer; their engagement celebration, done at a professional studio, him seated, with Sam's arms wrapped around him from behind; and their favourite wedding shot, a candid one taken by a friend, where Sam had tripped over something—

he couldn't remember what—and he'd grabbed her around the waist to steady her. Both of them were laughing with the joy of the day, her veil billowing around them like a benediction.

So she hadn't forgotten. If there was a man in her life, she'd have put the visible reminders of her past in a drawer, where they belonged.

"So why were you talking cranky?"

Brett dragged his attention back to his daughter. All he wanted right now was to take Sam into his arms, to comfort and love her. But he wouldn't even get to his feet without making a total fool of himself; reaching the floor for Casey had taken all the strength he'd had for now.

Maybe his therapist had been right—he wasn't physically ready for this. But the screaming need for his wife and daughter—to find and be with *his* family—had overruled the good sense that he, as a doctor, had. But he'd ached to see his child, to know his own flesh and blood—and he'd *needed* Sam so bad…

He hadn't expected this to be so damn *painful*. This was his family, yet they were strangers to him. And the worst part was, he no longer knew if he could blame Sam completely for that.

How did he feel about the child standing before

him, speaking so gravely and politely, like an old lady? He only wished he could feel anything right now but turbulent confusion. "Things get complicated sometimes, Casey. I don't know if I can explain it."

Casey stood still for a few moments, then she yawned. "Mummy says it's not nice to yell at people. You can talk nicely even when you're cranky."

"Mummy's right," he agreed, hiding a smile. "I'm sorry, Casey."

"'S'all right. I'm going back to bed now." She rubbed her eyes. "Good night, Mummy." She held out her arms.

Sam moved past him to gather her daughter into her arms. "Good night, princess. Love you." She kissed the feathery curls.

"Love you, too, Mummy." Casey began walking into her room.

"Good night, Casey." Brett quietly reminded her of his presence.

Casey turned back, smiling in his direction. "Good night, Mr. Glennon. It was nice meeting you. Maybe you can visit another time?"

Brett opened his mouth, then closed it. Brett Glennon, used to getting his way with determination or charm, had just been routed by a five-year-old. She didn't need to tell him how she felt; calling him Mr. Glennon told him all he didn't want to know.

Casey closed the door quietly behind her, but it felt as if she'd slammed it in his face.

"*Daddy* is an earned title—she doesn't know you yet. She'll get used to you if you're around long enough." Sam broke into his thoughts unerringly.

He turned to face her. "I will be around—count on it. She's my daughter," he rasped.

"Good. Then we're in agreement that we want to do what's best for her?"

"Yes, of course," he agreed, but with wariness. He could tell she was leading up to something, and some of his viler experiences in Africa had taught him to listen to the full proposal before he agreed to anything.

"Then we don't raise our voices again, no matter how upset we are. Casey has enough to adjust to without hearing her parents arguing." She smiled, though it was laden with emotional exhaustion. "That wasn't an accusation. I started the yelling tonight."

Willing to come to the party, he said, "Agreed. No raised voices." Tonight had been hard on both of them. He couldn't judge how much she'd changed based on an hour's conversation and reactions rooted in shock.

No matter what else he disagreed with, she was right on one point: Casey was—or should be—their first priority.

He felt a piercing shaft of bittersweet tenderness. *Casey.* She was part of him and Sam, an abiding reminder of their brief time of love, and she was such a gorgeous kid. It wasn't fair that she should be…be…

"Casey won't sleep if she can hear us. She has amazing hearing and insatiable curiosity. Come out here." After handing him his cane, she picked up the coffee mugs and led the way into the kitchen. She put the mugs down in the sink and had washed them by the time he managed to find a balance against the table and push himself upward to stand again, using the back of the chaise for balance. He hated using the cane to help him walk, even if he only had to use it for another six months to a year, as his therapist prognosticated.

Bring on next year, a healed knee and my surgical residency at the Royal Melbourne…

He was going crazy being so inactive. Three

days a week as a locum for a general practice just didn't keep his interest. He'd always wanted to be a surgeon once his tenure in Africa was done— and a minor inconvenience like a shattered patella and a shredded ligament wasn't going to get in his way for long.

Then it hit him: Sam had left him to it, instinctively knowing he didn't want help to stand.

It was more than anyone else except the therapists had known. His mother, frail as she was, continually picked up after him, no matter how many times he told her he had to do it himself to regain flexibility. Meghan, his sister, clucked over him like a mother hen, irritating him to snarling point—but the teary eyes and quavering, "We love you, Brett. We missed you so much," got him every time.

In some ways Sam knew him better than anyone ever had. She knew he'd want to deal with Casey alone. And she'd left him to get to his feet unaided, no matter that it hurt like hell. Though obviously she was far from rich, she hadn't asked for a cent from his wealthy parents, and asked for nothing from him now. She used no guilt trips on him to get her way, and never had—

My God, he thought as the revelation hit him.

She hadn't even used her pregnancy or her threatened miscarriage to get me to come home.

Brave, beautiful Sam. All alone, she just hadn't even asked for help from the one who'd taken vows to look after her in sickness and in health.

It seemed she wasn't the only one who'd failed that vow—and she'd had damn good reason to have broken it. More human lives hinged on their decisions six years ago than he'd thought.

Fragile, brave and honest, Sam had turned his world upside down from first glance…and she was still doing it without even trying. From the first night they met, she'd taken all his truths about women, his cynicism and have-fun-and-I-might-call-you attitudes, and knocked them on their heads. In all their time together, she hadn't asked anything from him but for him to love her.

Filled with a new suspicion, he headed out to the kitchen. "Did you know—or suspect—that you were pregnant before I left for Africa?"

The clatter of the mug she was drying, the soft rose colour creeping up her neck, gave him the answer she wouldn't speak aloud.

He closed his eyes, swearing to himself. This was insane. He'd come here to accuse Sam, to get the truth from her. He'd needed to know *why* she'd run from Melbourne, why she'd stayed safely in Australia while he'd almost died too many times to count. He'd been beaten, held at gunpoint, shot, starved and used as a medical slave, working for hours and even days without rest and with minimal food.

Sam hadn't been through any of that, damn it! So why did he feel as though he was the villain in a drama for which he hadn't received his lines?

He couldn't take any more; he felt more wrung out than the dishcloth Sam had just put away. "I'll call a cab." He pulled out his phone and dialed Information for the number. "I'm staying at the Rosemount in Parramatta if you need anything."

Silence for a moment; then, "Thank you," was all she said. He was grateful for her restraint. So much she could say and didn't—for instance, that she and Casey needed nothing from him.

"I'll be back tomorrow. What time would be convenient to take Casey—" He watched her spin around on him, and held his hand up as the auto-mated operator kicked in at the other end of the phone line. "To the park—with you, of course," he mouthed. As she'd said, they were Casey's parents and they couldn't afford to argue around her.

She relaxed and smiled a little, holding both hands up, all fingers, then two more.

He nodded and gave his attention to the automated call centre. After repeating the name of the taxi company three times, he rolled his eyes. "Finally I'm getting a human," he mouthed.

For answer, she held up her address book. The company's number was listed there. She'd had it all the time. She was smiling—no, she was laughing, and *damn,* it felt good to see it, even if her little joke wasn't particularly funny. As good as it had felt to have had her back in his arms tonight, responding to his touch with the same white-hot fire.

Thank you, oh, thank you, God—she still wanted him. That much about Sam hadn't changed, at least. Even in shock, she wanted him.

Where they went from here, he didn't know. All he knew was that, for the sake of their daughter—if not for the shadow of remembered love refusing to budge—he'd do his damnedest to make a phoenix rise from the ashes of the love they'd shared. He refused to give up on his marriage. He'd meant every word of his vow—

Except that I wasn't there for her in sickness, or in health. I wasn't there when she needed me the most. I broke my vow within two months—and she'd already been abandoned so many times, by her parents who dumped her at the orphanage, and then all the foster parents she had.

Such a fool. Why hadn't he *seen* that? He'd been so focused on the needs of people half a world away, he'd missed the needs of his bride. They'd only known each other two months when they'd married, and he'd gone within two months of their wedding. Yet somehow he'd thought Sam cured of all her insecurities. She'd had some terrible issues with meeting his family, and had never really let them into her life or heart. She didn't trust them to love her. Throughout her entire life, she'd never trusted her secrets or her heart to anyone but him.

And then, having gained her love and trust, I abandoned her for what I wanted to do, thinking my love was enough to have cured her.

All these years, so much pain, and it was only now he could see the sacrifices Sam had made so he could have his dream…and shame seared him. Had he always thought of her as his satellite? He'd known her fears, her pain and never knowing her parents and the bouts of uncontrollable sickness when she remembered the bad times in her childhood; but had he ever known her hopes, her dreams and needs? Looking back now, he doubted it. He'd moulded her into *his* life, giving her love for an all too brief time, then he'd disappeared.

Was she right to believe he'd only wanted her for what she'd given him?

What did Sam think he wanted from Casey?

He'd had two years of searching to think about their being together again; she'd barely had two hours of knowing he was even alive. All the wanting in the world couldn't change that fact. Sam needed time, and for once he'd put Sam first. And he needed time, as well. They'd both changed. They needed to adjust, and not just to each other. The family dynamics had transformed forever this day. Expectation was reality, and Sam had been alone with Casey for too many years.

It was time—way beyond time—that he learned what his wife's needs were…and if *he* could be what she needed.

"I'll get out of your hair." About to leave the kitchen, he leaned forward—using the cane so he didn't make a damn fool of himself by falling at her feet—and brushed her lips with his. "Good night, Sam. See you tomorrow."

She didn't answer him, but the uncertainty in her wide eyes and the sweet blush rising on her cheek was all the answer he wanted.

As he slowly made his way into the cab, he vowed that soon he'd have her back in his life, his arms and his bed, where he wanted her.

Wanted? Had to have, needed, was closer to the truth. Within two hours Sam had overturned his world a second time. With a look, a smile, tears and withholding of her normal devastating honesty, she'd taken years of anger and resentment and put them on hold. With a single kiss she'd taken his ambivalence and put in its place...*need.*

He'd seen this phenomenon many times as a doctor. He'd always wondered how people allowed themselves to turn into shivering wrecks, willing to lie, cheat, steal or even kill for the sake of their next fix of whatever substance made them forget the hell their life had become.

But that was what Sam was to him. She was his addiction, his greatest weakness and yet his most abiding strength. All that got him through the agonizing years he'd existed without her was the thought that he'd have her back in his arms, in his bed and in his heart. He wanted her as his wife again—in every way possible.

He'd always thought he was the strong one, and Sam needed *him*. But no matter how much she'd changed, he *needed* Sam so damn bad he was shaking with it.

Something had happened to Sam that she wasn't telling him. He had to make her talk, but it was as if he'd lost that ability with her when he needed it most. She was refusing to let him use their volcanic sexuality to get closer to her—and he wouldn't use it if he could, not before he'd gained her trust. As she'd said, sex wasn't the answer—it wasn't and never would be enough.

Am I enough? Can I ever be enough for Sam, the man I am now? Can I be a good father to Casey or will I screw that relationship up, too?

Whatever she was hiding wouldn't come out until she'd had time to get used to him being alive and back in her life…and Casey's life.

Casey was the one open door Sam couldn't shut on him. If he could gain his daughter's trust and love, surely they could become a family…and only he and God knew how damn much he needed that gift. Years and years of emptiness, knowing he'd left behind the one thing in his life that kept him steady. And *safe*. Without Sam—

The vision came to his mind like a newsreel, one

image after the other, haunting him constantly…families torn apart by loss and war, children orphaned, women and men wandering around like lost sheep seeking their shepherd because their partners had been kidnapped or killed.

Like a compass pointing south, his life was all wrong. *He* was wrong without Sam. Without his family he was as lost as those people in Mbuka.

The screaming pain in his head left him groping in emotional darkness. The dream—damn it, the dream was coming again. Inevitability stared him in the face: this was life as he knew it, and maybe how he'd always know it. Getting home to Sam, his tunnel-vision focus, hadn't taken the agony away, hadn't made everything go back to the way things were before.

Would he ever be normal again? Did he have anything left inside his damaged heart to give to his beautiful, fragile daughter, let alone to Sam?

Would he make their lives better? Or would he, just by being here, destroy them as surely as he'd torn his knee and his future career into shattered pieces?

Sam tossed in her bed, lying wide-eyed and sleepless. The storm had passed quickly in a show of fierce light and thunder, with very little rain to clear the pulsing heat of the night. Her skin felt fevered, burning, her body restless—and even a thousand laps in the pool was no longer a cooling option.

Memories were no longer hers alone; Casey was involved now. But she couldn't allow Brett to get too close to her, because he had the power still to break her heart, body and soul.

She sighed and rolled over again, but her whirling mind and pounding heart prevented rest. She'd seen it in his eyes, seen the moment he'd turned everything around on her and taken control. The hunter was back—and he wasn't hunting Casey. He wanted *her*…

Well, hardly any surprise there. They'd always been like a firestorm in bed, unstoppable, unquenchable and not in want—it was that need for what came with the loving: the *love*.

I've never felt this deeply about anyone, Sam. I love you so much.

She punched the pillow. She'd spent every day of the past six years fighting the memories! Why, *why* had he come back just when she'd thought she'd been starting to win?

No other man had ever had a chance to come close. Casey was first, last and everything; her child filled every corner of her heart. No man would ever come between them.

Be honest—no man could compete with Brett. He knocked you off your feet with one look.

A shiver raced through her, hot and delicious. Brett was the most exquisite disaster to ever have befallen her, robbing her of her icy barriers and making her *live,* even when she hadn't wanted to. Even when she'd grieved for him, she hadn't regretted a moment of her love.

Now he was back. And along with his damaged body and soul, he was as needing and as commanding as ever—and though that terrified her, he'd given her Casey to love, the most incredible gift of her life. She couldn't lock him out now if she tried—not even if his ultimate agenda was to take Casey to Melbourne with him, to take custody of his only child.

It was pointless to hide anymore. Somehow she had to come to terms with the changes that had come to her safe, comfortable world…and keep Casey with her.

The only way was to run again. But as Brett had shown her with a few poignant words, this wasn't about her life or security. She knew what it was to live without family, without love—and she could deny nothing to her beautiful girl that she deserved.

Including the love of the Glennon family?

The thought of it made her want to throw up, but now they knew Casey was blind, they could find her with ease no matter how often or how far she ran. The facilities Casey needed were listed in every phone book.

She felt the end of her tranquil life in Sydney coming toward her as surely as she'd felt the storm coming earlier. She would do what was best for Casey—but she would also do whatever was necessary to protect her own heart. He was injured now, home to recuperate. How long would he hang around before he needed to go and save the world again, leaving her vulnerable to another lawsuit by his parents?

She couldn't believe he was home to stay; she knew she lacked the personality that made people love her for life. From her parents to foster parents, friends, to Brett's parents and even Brett, she had learned one vital lesson: sooner or later, everyone left her. But if the Glennons managed to gain custody of Casey, her reason to live would be taken from her.

She had to stop him from taking Casey to

Melbourne for as long as she could. And since she refused to rob Brett of his faith in his parents' goodness and love, there was only one way: she must lock him out of her bedroom—and out of a renewed storm upon her battered heart.

She couldn't afford to let herself love him again, because if she did, she'd lose all she'd ever had to live for.

CHAPTER FOUR

"Why did Mr. Glennon come here, Mummy?"

It was the question Sam had been asking all through the long, sleepless night. Her quiet, ordered life had been turned upside down within moments of his arrival.

Just like the first time.

Love at first sight. Until she met Brett, she'd thought it romantic hooey. How could anyone love someone they didn't know?

Yet the magic had shimmered between them from the first glance.

At twenty-two, six years out of the final foster home, eight out of the orphanage, Sam had had few friends and trusted none of them. She'd let no man anywhere near her body or her heart; she'd been known as the Ice Princess by the men at Montgomery Partners. She'd never put love in her equation until the moment she'd looked up into the laughing golden-brown eyes of the man who'd taken her heart moments after he'd taken his shoes off. Love really did happen like that.

"Mummy?"

Sam shook herself. "He came to see you." But that wasn't the whole truth.

Casey's thoughtful nod told Sam she was processing every word, and pain was already slicing through her for the next inevitable question. "Why didn't he come afore? Was he 'shamed 'cause I'm blind, Mummy?"

Oh, dear God, how life repeats; Casey was her daughter and had inherited her hang-ups. "No, Casey," she replied in a shaking voice, holding her precious girl tight. "He lived a long way away. And you remember how you said he walked funny? He was sick for a long time."

"Okay." Casey smoothed out the blue floral dress with the pink sash and the matching pink headband in her hair, letting her curls tumble around her face in a silver-gold halo. "Does Mr. Glennon think I'm pretty?"

"You bet he does."

Sam twisted around to see Brett leaning in the open doorway, smiling.

And though the smile was for Casey, Sam's heart began racing. In the jeans of the night before and an Australian Rules Football jersey—his favourite team, Collingwood—Brett looked like any dad ready to take his child to the park…but oh, so much sexier.

He walked in the door, leaned against the back of the sofa—he obviously hated the cane, for he used it as little as possible—and inspected his daughter with a teasing grin.

She can't see it, Sam thought in turbulent confusion and a sudden flash of compassion for hyperactive Brett's descent into slow, painful movement. *You can't impress her with your smile!*

But when he said, "What a gorgeous girl I've got!" the smile came through in his voice. To Sam's disbelief, Casey responded to his blatant flirting, blushing and giggling. "I'll be beatin' the boys off with my handy daughter-protection baseball bat on our date."

Casey's head tilted, her eyes sparkling. "What's a date?"

Leaning on the cane, he walked over to her. With the same difficulty as the night before, he struggled to hunker down beside Casey. His damaged leg stuck out at an awkward angle. "A date is when a man and a woman go somewhere together because they want to."

Come with me to see the fireworks on the river at midnight, Sam, he'd said that first night at the party, minutes after their first kiss. *Let's escape these stuffed shirts. Walk along the Yarra River barefoot with me. We'll have hot chocolate, wander around, hold hands and kiss. Come with me because it's irresponsible and fun. Come because it makes no sense. Come because it's still a wonderful, beautiful world. Come with me because you want to.*

The bittersweetness of that first date lanced through her with slicing pain. She always avoided walking along waterways now; seeing loving couples hurt too much.

"I'm not a woman," Casey pointed out, her hands reaching out to find the cause of Brett's physical difficulty. She'd heard the hitching in his movements and the limp, accentuated by the soft clunk of the cane, as he'd crossed the room.

"Let me recheck the official rule book for dating." He rustled a paper in his pocket. "Aha…clause 347a states clearly that a beautiful girl may take the place of a woman in the absence of same…if she wants to."

Casey had found the cane he'd put behind him, feeling along its length. and Sam waited for the inquisition. Casey had insatiable curiosity and didn't know the meaning of the word *no*. But obviously he'd diverted her with his nonsense. "You're laughing, Mr. Glennon. I can hear it in your voice."

Sam watched the shadow cross Brett's face every time Casey named him, but he answered her in the same lighthearted vein. "Hey, dates don't call each other by their last names, kiddo."

An enchantingly shy smile flitted across the little girl's face, and Brett's heart ached anew. Casey had such possibilities. She was intelligent, graceful, beautiful. She could grace the catwalks of the world one day with her luminous beauty—

If she didn't fall flat on her face going down the catwalk. If I could fix that—

"Then what'll I call you?" Casey was asking.

He hesitated for a moment before he plunged in. "Daddy sounds good to me if it does to you," he said gruffly, aching for family connection.

Wishing for the moon, obviously. Casey's smile faded at the mere word. Her hand froze over the walking stick she was still fingering; her head drooped as if she were embarrassed.

He glanced up at Sam, who mouthed, "Fix it, Brett!" Obviously she was as alarmed as Casey by his suggestion that he become part of the family.

Feeling flattened, he said quietly, "But Brett will be fine for now, kiddo."

Clearly relieved by the lifting of the pressure he'd put on her, Casey brightened. "I'd like to go on a date with you, Brett."

Ridiculous to feel such relief at her acceptance, but he did. *Take one step at a time with her. Baby steps,* he thought wryly.

Damn it, he had to stop dreaming for more with this family reunion. He'd invested his every hope on this time and, in doing so, had put too much expectation onto them both. He had a chance to know Casey—and to truly know Sam. Given his self-realisations last night, it was probably more than he deserved right now.

He now knew he hadn't been a good husband to Sam—and that was *before* he'd been left a half man by his experiences in Africa. What made him think he could be a good enough father to Casey?

Just keep your fears and dreams to yourself and be grateful for what you have.

"Let's go." He swept open the door.

Sam moved to take Casey's hand as she

headed out the door, but, acting on the gut instinct that had saved his life in Mbuka, Brett held her back. "Off you go, kiddo. Meet us at the gate."

Sam stared at him as if he'd grown another head. "She can't walk to the car alone!"

He frowned at her, trying to work out why. "Haven't you taught her how many steps to the gate?"

"Of course I have…"

"And you've never let her do it? *At five?*" One of the first things he'd learned from the Deaf and Blind Children's Centre was to teach the kids as much independence as they could handle, as early as possible, in case of emergency. They needed to know what to do in case their parents were sick or knocked out—the knowledge should be drilled into them. Surely five wasn't too young for Casey to know how to reach her own gate?

What other basics had Sam kept Casey from knowing…and why? *Why* would she not want Casey to be as strong and independent as possible?

Sam's gaze dropped. Her mouth turned down. And Casey stood still, waiting and listening.

Knowing the enormous risk he took—for he was a stranger to Casey and the interloper in

Sam's world—he said to his daughter, "Hey, kiddo, wait for us at the gate. You can do that all by yourself, can't you?"

"Sure I can. Watch me, Brett!" Casey's chest puffed out; her dimpled grin flashed on him as she turned around. Holding on to the rail, she counted down three stairs, then carefully she paced one step after the other.

Baby steps...like father, like daughter. In more ways than one. It seemed he could learn a lot from his daughter about caution and knowing limits.

Sam shook off his hand, straining forward, checking the path. "Casey, watch out for—"

Having already checked to see there was nothing in the way, Brett had to act before Sam destroyed Casey's first taste of confidence. He swept Sam into his arms. His lips muffled any panicked protest she was about to make. Sam melted against him, just as she always had.

Baby steps, Glennon. Don't force her into something you may not be ready for either.

So he kissed Sam with a tenderness that muddled her mind and left her shaking.

And as he kissed his wife, a tiny girl walked down her front path alone for the first time, her pale, spiritual face glowing with accomplishment.

* * *

"Whee! Look at me, Mummy! Look at me!"

Her fragile baby was on an unprotected swing, being pushed until she was soaring with the pink-and-grey galahs wheeling overhead.

"Lovely, darling," Sam called, her voice faint.

Why had she agreed to Brett's request that this be *his* day with Casey? Oh, she knew. Her agreement came from her guilt at his lost years with Casey. And he was a doctor—he knew how to keep her little girl safe from harm.

But the main reason was the depth of pain in his eyes as he'd asked—and the utter longing as he'd looked at his child. Brett was a stranger to his daughter—a daughter whose love and joy in life could have helped him through his darkest days…

It was my fault, all my fault.

But with one word—*yes*—she'd lost control. Instead of the quiet local park Casey was familiar with, they'd come to a rambling old playground he'd seen on the outskirts of Parramatta, the major shopping centre west of Sydney. It had about a dozen preschoolers playing here, and Brett seemed to think that all those strangers gawking at the blind kid was a bonus.

Instead of walking Casey through the steps it

would take to each piece of equipment, he let her count it herself and called out when she was three steps from connection or from another child. Though Sam knew this was the best method, she'd never been able to bring herself to use it—especially in public. She always told herself, *When she's a bit older. She's not ready.*

She came back to the present to find Brett beside her. "Casey wanted to slow the swing down by herself."

Sam jumped up to go to her, but he held her back, gently bearing her down until she sat. "This is my day with Casey. I'm her father. I'd never allow her to injure herself."

Fretting, she fumed, "You don't know what could happen—"

"I'm a doctor," he reminded her, his eyes intent. "I've checked the place out. Casey's safe enough from anything but a cut knee."

"What?" Sam cried. "She hurt herself?"

"Of course not," he said gently, touching her hand and sending sweet, warm shivers all the way through her. "I'm watching her. She's safe, Sam. Have a rest. Enjoy the sunshine and let me get to know my daughter. Let her get to know me."

Slowly she nodded. "All right."

"Thank you." He smiled and feathered a light kiss across her mouth, sending ripples of pleasure through her entire body. "I won't let you down."

She barely heard the words. As with the kiss earlier, he was seducing her into complete muddleheadedness with a single touch. Turning her from the single-minded mother into a woman aching for more than she had—more than she deserved from him. How could he want her after she'd robbed him of his own child? He still didn't know the reason she'd left Melbourne—but he seemed to be taking her on trust.

Which is more than I do for him.

"Brett—" She stopped, confused. What did she say—*don't touch me,* when it had to be pathetically obvious how much she wanted him to touch her? "I...don't—" With a sigh, she said softly, "You're pushing too fast. You're here for Casey, not me."

"Am I?" With darkened eyes and a deep frown, he turned toward Casey, who was heading for the roundabout. "Good girl, Casey, keep going. Another six steps," he called to her. He leaned on his cane, watching as she found the roundabout, wanting to work out how to make this alien piece of play equipment go around without getting help. "Leave one foot on the roundabout, one foot kicking off from the ground, kiddo. Go slow to start and hang on with both hands!"

Casey grinned and obeyed him with a wide smile of discovery on her heart-shaped face as she made the equipment obey her.

Brett turned back to Sam, his face awed. "She's amazing, isn't she? It's hard to believe she can't see, with the confidence she has with new experiences. I can't believe anything so perfect, so beautiful, is mine. If...if only..." He shook his head and limped over to Casey.

Sam knew what he didn't say; she'd thought it a thousand times herself. Pride and joy and love mixed with the wistful *if onlys,* the constant ache, the wishing that this special, adorable child could have all life's experiences and not be limited by her one imperfection.

Seeing her deepest wish reflected in Brett's eyes was a burden shared...and yet it was dangerous. His understanding her pain, her *need* was too dangerous. And whenever he flashed that warm, intimate smile at her, the fragile woman began emerging from a six-year chrysalis, leaving her *aching* for him to kiss her again...

In less than twenty-four hours, he'd sent her world spinning. He was taking over before she'd begun to come to terms with his being alive. He'd ripped all her comfortable certainties from her— her illusions of safety gone in moments last night; her mothering skills questioned after an hour in the park. And the worst part was that she *knew* he was right.

At the moment, he was terrifying her, bouncing the seesaw so Casey jumped whenever she reached the top. But it made Casey laugh hysterically. "More, Brett, more!"

He allowed her to slide down the slide alone and he didn't even catch her at the base, letting her land with a thump, breathless and laughing, into the sandpit below. "Can I do that again?"

After a half hour of torture, Sam called out, "I think she's had enough, Brett!"

All she received for her forbearance was a cry of protest. "Aw, Mummy, I wanna play with Brett. I never had such fun before!"

Stabbed with the careless wound, she glared at the instigator. His smile in return was both sympathetic and insecure, as if he understood that she was hiding tears beneath her anger—and as if he knew part of her wished he'd never found them.

Perhaps he did know. He knew her as no one else had ever bothered to in her life.

He'd been the only one outside government departments who'd heard her story. During those long, hot nights after lovemaking on their honeymoon, when he'd drawn her out on her starved, loveless childhood from her locked heart, piece by faltering piece—

Don't think about it.

Brett landed in on her thoughts with a *whoosh,* as he thumped down beside her. "Whew," he muttered, wiping his heated brow. "She's one busy kid."

"Where is she?" Sam cried, searching frantically until she saw Casey climbing the ladder to the slide.

"Seven stairs up. She counts very well for five. I suppose she's had to. Don't sweat it, Sam; she's with a friend."

"But she doesn't know anyone. How could she—"

"Calm down, angel," he said softly. "Kids make friends with other kids all the time. It's a natural part of life."

Sam stared at him, taken aback. She'd always carefully vetted every child Casey had played with, as well as their parents. "What if they find out she's blind?"

Brett smiled a little. "They know, Sam—mother and daughter. The little girl has slowed down so Casey can keep up and is holding her hand everywhere."

Squinting against the bright summer sunshine, Sam saw it was true. The mother watched every move Casey and her daughter made. When she noticed Sam's anxious inspection, she gave her a friendly smile and wave, indicating to her to relax.

Sam watched with anxious care for the next ten minutes, until the other child brought out her Barbie dolls, giving Casey time to feel her way around them and the clothing. Then they sat on the ground and played mothers and babies.

Just like normal children.

She remembered doing just that herself once, during six months in one of her foster homes. She'd made a friend at school, Lyndal, who'd been as extroverted as Sam had been cripplingly shy. Lyndal had invited her home most days and taught her the joys of make-believe and "teenage" dolly-romance with Barbies and Kens.

Then she'd been returned to the orphanage. Her foster mother had had heart trouble and her foster father hadn't been able to cope with a child as well as a sick wife.

Something shifted inside her; tears rushed to her eyes. She turned away before Brett could see them. "I need to do some shopping," she said, trying to control the quivering huskiness in her voice. She couldn't think of the reasons why she shouldn't leave her precious girl with Brett. All she knew was that she had to get away—from the pain, from the things she was feeling and from their instigator. She had to run from Brett. "I'll be back in an hour."

"I'm not trying to upset you, Sam. I just want Casey and me to get to know each other our own way. I'm not asking anything more."

Yet. The word hovered there between them. No matter what he said, they both knew father-daughter time wasn't all he wanted…and *more* took on unbearable proportions when his family came into the equation.

With a start, she realised she hadn't thought of the Glennons all morning. The desperate need to escape was from Brett alone.

"I have to go," she said. Her voice was husky, almost a whisper.

"I'll drive you," he volunteered in the quiet voice he used to use when he'd known she was remembering her childhood and he couldn't help her with anything but his presence and his un-questioning love.

The love she couldn't allow to happen again.

"No! I—I…" She got to her feet, almost as desperate to run away as she'd been six years ago to get out of Melbourne. "There's a bus due in a few minutes that takes me right to the mall. And for once I can shop without Casey asking for half the chocolate counter. Since you're here, I might as well make use of you."

"You don't need to worry that I'll take her out of the state while you're gone," he said, his voice restrained yet filled with quiet reassurance. "Casey doesn't even know me yet."

Obviously he remembered how she'd always run from too much emotion. *Damn* him for knowing that about her. She tried to laugh it off. "I wasn't scared of that. I'm not the emotional train wreck I used to be, Brett."

But if she thought he'd see through the bravado, she was wrong. "That much is obvious. You've changed, Sam. You've grown."

You're not the girl I fell in love with.

The words he hadn't spoken shivered in the air between them. And though she'd told herself she and Casey were a complete unit and she didn't need his love to make her whole and strong, somehow his words hurt even more.

"I'd better see if Casey will let me go. I've never left her with anyone before except at school and the Centre."

But, she discovered without surprise, Casey didn't mind. She had Kimberley to play Barbies with, and once she knew Brett would stay with her, she had only one concern. "I want a Kinder Surprise, Mummy, or a Yowie. They're the chocolates with the toys inside 'em."

"Sure, princess," she said, trying to keep the choking tears from her voice. She turned her face from Brett's before his pity and her own terror-filled longings overwhelmed her.

Within a day, Sam had gone from the centre of Casey's being to the purchaser of chocolate. Just one day ago, part of her had been longing for space, for time to be *Sam,* not just Mummy. Now, thanks to Brett, she had it.

She bolted toward the bus stop without looking back.

CHAPTER FIVE

Turning in the drive at Sam's house, Brett knew he'd blown it with Sam big-time today. The only thing he couldn't figure out was how.

The problem wasn't with Casey. Forget baby steps—after today he was galloping straight into the kid's heart with every new piece of fun he gave her. But Sam didn't speak all the way home except to answer Casey. She seemed to be either on the verge of tears or an outburst of fury, and none of it was aimed at their daughter.

Yes, folks, we're in for a great bout tonight, he thought wryly. *A full twelve rounds with the champ, Sam Glennon, and she's not in the mood for preliminaries!*

Casey was yawning mightily by the time they reached home, after stuffing herself at the pizza house Brett had chosen for dinner. "I had such fun today, Mummy," she sighed as her mother tucked her into bed. "Can we do it again tomorrow?"

"You have your swimming lesson at the Centre tomorrow, princess," Sam replied in a constricted tone. "Angela would miss you."

"Oh." Casey pouted. "I s'pose so. The next day?"

"Tell you what, sweetie. How about we picnic at home and have a swim?"

Tears filled Casey's eyes; her lips quivered. "Wanna go out with Brett! I want—"

"How about I drive you to the Centre, kiddo?" Brett interrupted the burgeoning tantrum. "I can meet your friends."

Casey said grudgingly, not yet mollified with the compromise, "All right. But why are you so cranky, Mummy? Didn't you have fun today?"

Brett watched the conflicting emotions on his wife's face and took pity on her. "How about we read a story together before bed?"

Casey immediately bounced up in bed, throwing the sheet off. "Yeah! I want the one about the magic broom!"

Sam passed him the book with a guilty, worried look. The book was in Braille.

But with a smile, Brett fingered the title page.

"Whoa—*Miss Missy's Magic Mop.* What a cool name for a book! I can't wait to read it."

A strangled sound came from behind him. As he turned, grinning with the fantastic surprise he'd been keeping for this moment, Sam turned and left the room looking devastated.

Brett frowned. What now? Back in Melbourne, while waiting for her address, he'd thought learning Braille would be the perfect way to connect with Casey. Surely it told Sam he was ready and willing—more than willing—to tackle fatherhood with a special-needs child?

Casey was asleep by the time he finished reading, teaching her the words from the story.

He laid the book on the floor, looking at his daughter. Her flyaway curls framed her face like a halo. She looked like a tiny piece of crafted porcelain.

This is my daughter, my child.

Something tugged at his chest, something soft, warm and fuzzy. He smiled at her, pushing an errant curl from her face.

"Put the book away. She could trip over it when she wakes up."

The challenge had been thrown. *Okay, folks, round one!* Meekly enough, he put it away.

Then he limped into the living room, one brow raised in wry amusement. "Off you go, angel. Give me the lowdown on everything I did wrong today."

Faced with the opportunity she'd been seething for all afternoon, the wind left her sails. "I don't know what to say." She closed her eyes.

"What's the problem, Sam? Casey's a great kid and she likes me already—"

"Of course she likes you while you're buttering her up with pony rides and McDonald's." Sam sighed. "You thought I was jealous, didn't you?" She looked up, devastated, lost. "Perhaps I was. I'm not used to sharing her. But you're not giving me time to get used to it—especially when you become her instant hero. She's too young to understand the concept of rich and poor." She sighed. "I'm not a Glennon, Brett. Renting this house, paying bills and putting food on the table takes almost everything I've got. Tell me how I cope with her demands for more of the same when you head back to Melbourne?"

"I'm not—" Then her words hit him and stopped him dead—and all his assurance for future financial and emotional assistance would do nothing at this point.

Oh, man, he'd really blown it big-time. He'd always despised "weekend dads" who spoiled their kids rotten and sent them back to the mother for discipline. A ton of them had come into the emergency rooms when he'd been an intern and a resident doctor. He'd had to deal with kids sick on a weekend diet of junk food and exhausted from too much fun, with harassed second-weekend dads demanding he fix the kids before the ex-wives found out and tore strips off them.

To his shame, Brett had fallen into the same trap without thinking, and with exactly the same excuse. *I just want my kids to love me, to know I love them. I want to make up for not seeing them twelve days out of fourteen…*

Or five years out of five.

When he'd come storming up here, he'd barely thought beyond his driving need to meet his daughter, catch up on five years, make up for his unintentional neglect. So he'd studied Braille, read all the latest information on what was best for blind children, visited the Melbourne Centre dozens of times and taken all the classes he could sign on for. He'd believed himself ready to prove to Sam he'd be a good father…and husband.

Casey was *his* child, *his* daughter, a Glennon stripped of her rightful due—

But he hadn't counted on Casey as a reality or thought of her as a person.

Last night, seeing a depth of pain in Sam he'd never expected and coming head-on against Casey's unintentional distance from him, he'd had his blinders torn off. Lost in his own needs and accusations, he hadn't thought of what Sam had been through, bringing up a special-needs child alone and believing herself a widow. She'd had to make her own way and she'd done so with lack of complaint and a lot of love.

But her words just now were far more telling than any confusion or rejection she'd given thus far. *I'm not a Glennon, Brett.*

She didn't feel married to him anymore.

During a sleepless night in which he'd been afraid to sleep in case the dreams of Mbuka came again and the victims' faces in the dreams became those of his wife and child, he'd decided to break down those barriers with a battering ram. He'd *make* Casey like him—that'd show Sam that he'd be a good dad.

The Braille and his knowledge of Casey's need for basic independence were supposed to be the icing on the cake. *See what a great father I can be, Sam? So give me my life back, the life I'd planned with you...*

Obviously those first-night blinders had been no more than partially torn off. With each passing hour, with each conversation with Sam, he only revealed more of his own inadequacies and showed himself just how far he had yet to go to gain Sam's trust.

"I'll fix it," he said, hiding his frustration at the emotional brick wall he kept running into with Sam and at the mistakes he'd made with Casey. "Tomorrow we go to the Centre. No presents, no excitement and no money—just father-daughter time. Okay?"

Sam nodded. Her delicate face, though in bright light, seemed hooded, shadowed with that withdrawal he was already beginning to hate. "Casey can't walk into your world like I did, Brett. For her sake, you have to walk into hers first."

Right. He could do that. But so far, whenever he tried to impress Sam with how well he could adapt, she put him in his place. As a father, she had no choice but to give him another chance; but as a husband or lover, her barricades were five miles high. And she didn't have a clue how much he needed to break them down, how much he needed *her,* ached to hold her in his arms at night to end the nightmare of being alone with his memories.

Somehow he'd hoped for divine intervention with Sam. He'd hoped to God that, with the miracle of her love, she could kill the vile dreams that walked with him night and day. He'd expected her to turn the emotional shipwreck he was now into the man he used to be. He wanted his life back, and Sam was the key.

But what does Sam want? What does she need? Has she got any time leftover from Casey to give me what I want? Can I give her what she needs?

Once again he'd come up against the hard questions, the ones he didn't have any answers for.

"I'd better go," he said abruptly. If he didn't leave now, he was going to do something *really* stupid, something pitiful and needy, like grab her and kiss her, make her want to take him to her bed. While it would slake a six-year hunger, it would only create a truckload of problems he'd have to deal with later. "What time should I come tomorrow?"

"Eight," she told him, sounding subdued. She was flipping her shoe on and off the foot, lost in contemplation, shutting him out again without conscious thought.

Obviously twenty-four hours wasn't enough to end her deep shock at his being alive. He'd been a damned fool to think or hope for more than the open door she'd shown him.

Maybe it was time to remind her that he was alive, that he *knew* her, without any painful inferences to the past she seemed determined to outrun.

He'd give *anything* to have his time over, to be the man he'd been…to have the Sam who'd adored him so blindly he'd felt like the king of the world in her presence, bathed in her love.

"Take the shoes off, Sam. You know you want to," he said with a grin, aiming for lightness. *Keep things simple and happy.*

Sam smiled at him with a touch of shyness and kicked off the slippers. "Better?"

He winked. "That's the Sam I know." He held back from adding words of love; not only would they frighten her, at this point he didn't have a clue if his love helped at all, while he was a limping, *needing* disaster. "I'd do the same, but I find it hard to kick anything these days. Just as well Casey's a girl. Kicking a football around with a boy would be beyond me."

She laughed, with a touch of relief threaded through it. She was as tired of the emotional drain as he was—while he had nightmares and physical pain, she had a special-needs child to cope with and six years of believing he was dead.

He had to keep reminding himself to give her time. Becoming Casey's dad was the key—and not making demands on her overloaded emotions and strength.

It was time to *show* her, not *impress* her—because right now he didn't know if she needed *anything* from him except to go away and never come back.

"Good night." He knew his gaze kissed her lips if his mouth didn't. And by the slow blush that filled her face as she murmured the same, she knew it as well as he did. But he didn't know if she wanted the touch as much as he did; she'd hooded her longing, if it existed. But she looked tense, sad and so damned *alone*...

Sam didn't know he'd moved toward her—she must have really been tired, because his cane made enough noise for a deaf person to hear—until his gentle kneading of her shoulder muscles had her blowing out a sigh of pleasure; she felt the tension headache ease. Without thinking, she leaned her head back against him, feeling a wave of calm wash over her. "Thank you."

"Anything for you," he whispered against her ear, making her shiver clear down to her toes.

"This isn't a good idea," she muttered, even as she went limp with muscle satisfaction and felt sweet, edging desire begin taking the place of stress.

"What, a massage? Or are you talking about this?" A fluttering butterfly kiss landed on the nape of her neck.

"Brett…" She could hear the longing in her voice; she was disgusted with herself but was unable to control the building fire inside her. "Oh, Brett…"

"Samantha." He drew her name out in that low, sexy way he had when he was aroused. "Come here."

His voice mesmerised her. She turned her face, lifting to his.

One of Brett's charms lay in the fact that he never did the expected. Sam, leaning back for a deep, hot kiss and a swift sweeping into his arms and to the bedroom, received a sweet kiss of such exquisite tenderness it brought tears to her eyes. It was like a first shy kiss of a boy and girl at a school dance or a party.

It was unlike any kiss he'd given her since that first one—or the first night they'd made love. That night had been slow and tender. He had known, with her abusive background, how hard it had been for her to give him her trust and he'd been terrified he wouldn't earn it but destroy it.

He kissed her as if she were still that scared, shivering girl.

He kissed away the tear trickling down her cheek. "I'm here for you, angel. I'm here."

She pulled back, searching his eyes. "For how long?" she whispered.

It was a question Brett didn't think he should answer, not yet. Sam wasn't any more ready to hear it than Casey was. "For the rest of Casey's life, I swear I'll be there for her. I'm her father. I want you to know I'll never leave her alone, no matter what happens with us." He felt his knee begin to give beneath him, and no wonder, after the day he'd had. He came around to sit beside her. He picked up her hand and twined his fingers through hers. "I want you, Sam. You have to know that," he began, unsure just how much to say.

But Sam pulled her hand from his, her eyes wary. "Don't touch me again. It's not fair."

Brett frowned. "To whom?"

She gazed at him with the sorrow of farewell. "To me—and more importantly to Casey."

He couldn't understand this at all. "Why?"

Her eyes fell to her lap. "When I knew Casey was blind, I made myself a promise. I'd never even start a relationship with a man who couldn't love Casey for who she is and accept her, blindness and all." Her hands twisted around each other. "I don't know if that's something you can do, Brett, even if you are her father. You had fun with her today, but it's not enough."

Stung, he returned, "I know there's more to being a father, but you're condemning me after twenty-four hours. How do I learn how to be a father in a day? How do I love someone I only met twenty-four hours ago?"

"I loved Casey in moments," she replied, quiet but the condemnation clear in her voice.

"You've known her since she was inside you. You've been with her before she was a newborn. I missed out on all that. Give me a chance to know her," he said forcefully.

He read volumes in the sorrow in her eyes. She'd give him the chance, but she didn't believe he'd make the grade, leaving him in a turmoil of confused betrayal. What had he done to make her think he'd be a bad father—

Besides the stupid mistakes I made today?

He sighed. "I'd really better go this time."

"Brett."

He turned back, pulse racing, half afraid of her words.

"I have to put her first." Her eyes pleaded with him to understand. "I know how it feels to have no one love or want you."

The utter forlornness on her face broke his will. He limped back to her and, dropping the hated cane, gathered her in his arms, inhaling her fresh scent, her cleanness, her—oh, God help him, her *everything* that was clean and innocent and beautiful, everything that didn't remind him of the vileness he was trying so damn hard to forget.

Sam, my sweet miracle, please come back to me and end my nightmare...

Having lost his gift of words in a bloody battlefield surgeon's tent somewhere in the darkest war-torn zones in Africa, he had no words he could think of that she'd accept. So he just held her, letting his duct-taped heart tell her what his clumsy mouth would only destroy.

Eventually she drew back. "Good night, Brett." Her voice was husky with tears, but the farewell was definite—and he felt pretty shaky himself.

He used his cane to get to his feet. At the door, he turned back for a moment. "One thing you need to know is that Casey's a secure kid. She knows she's loved."

Sam's smile came out like a half-faded rainbow after a rainstorm, elfin and elusive as the pot of gold at its end and just as beautiful. "Thank you."

Though he ached to touch her again, he made himself smile and shut the door behind him.

Throughout another sleepless night, Sam wondered if he'd deliver on his promise to be what Casey needed. Her precious child needed parents who'd focus on her needs, not enter into debates over every task Sam performed for her— or over whether Casey would meet the Glennons. She had no way of knowing whether Brett was here to *know* Casey or take her away.

She knew statistics said mothers often won custody cases—but there would likely be a court order for her to return to Melbourne to allow Casey access to her extended family. And David Glennon had threatened to prove her unfit in any way he could.

She and Brett barely knew each other. She couldn't expect his loyalty; it would lie with the family who'd loved and supported him…who'd believed he was alive when she'd cut and run.

What if he thought the Glennons would do a better job raising Casey than she had?

Was that why he'd countermanded all her rules for Casey's welfare today? Was he seeing her as a control freak stifling Casey? *Did that prove her an unfit mother?*

Had she deprived Casey of as normal a childhood as she deserved, filled with family and love, by running from Melbourne, not staying to fight the Glennons or make peace with them? God forgive her if her cowardice rebounded on Casey. If they took her reason to live from her...

She couldn't take the chance that Brett was the man she'd loved before. Though she'd seen momentary flashes of the man she'd fallen so deeply in love with, they disappeared too fast, and he'd become someone she didn't recognise.

There were too many ifs, too many maybes, too many unfounded hopes to make a decision. One day in a park did not make a father. A sweet kiss didn't rule out a deeper agenda. She could see it in his eyes; he hadn't said what he truly wanted beyond making love to his wife and having a little time to get to know Casey.

She didn't know if, even for Casey's sake, she should hope he'd become a true father, because then they'd have to face changing states, returning to the old life and the Glennon family. And that was a test she couldn't bear Casey to face— let alone herself.

CHAPTER SIX

"RIGHT, YOU'RE COMING up to it now. See the shopping mall on the right? The Centre's on the left. Turn in at the driveway."

Brett almost missed the designated driveway, staring at the lovely, mellow surrounds of the Deaf and Blind Children's Centre. He righted the car in time with a tiny screech, taking in the open grounds, the low brick buildings and colourful gardens with a reflective air.

"Expecting a prison, perhaps?"

Sam's mocking question had him grinning. "No. The Centre in Melbourne is pretty, too, but this feels so mellow."

He noted her narrow-eyed surprise at his reference but had no way of knowing if it was a reaction to his reference to visiting the Centre or to Melbourne itself. It didn't feel the right time to tell her how many times he'd visited the

Centre; with the way she'd been looking at him since she'd opened the door this morning, she might view it as points-scoring.

Casey piped up. "I like Glenmore Park better. It smells so good."

Brett turned a quizzical look on his wife.

Sam smiled. "Glenmore Park's where Casey attends her reverse-integration preschool, where kids from the local community learn beside those with challenges. Casey comes here only once a week to learn to swim and for occasional assessments."

"Why does Glenmore Park smell good?"

Sam smiled. "They've planted various herbs and scented flowers along the paths, to tell the kids where they are."

Even though he was a doctor and knew many institutes that went to great lengths to help their speciality patients, he found himself deeply impressed by the thoughtful insight into the kids' needs. "Why didn't they do the same here?"

Casey interrupted. "I'll show you what they do here, Brett. I'll take you to the pool."

Sam directed him around to the back of the Centre to a car park. "This one's our parking area."

He'd barely pulled up when Casey leaped out

and, finding the path with unerring accuracy, made an imperious gesture. "C'mon, Brett. Keep up."

Brett grinned. So, Casey wanted to show off her skills to him? "I'm coming." He cast a look of amused long-suffering over his shoulder. Sam laughed, but it seemed strained as she waved him on.

Casey took his hand and led him to the building where her teacher waited. She turned when the path did; when the path changed from cement to harder—scraping Pebblecrete that made swishing sounds beneath her feet—Casey pointed at one of the low brick buildings before them. "Here we are." As if she could see the woman waiting outside the building, she smiled and waved. "Hi, Angela!"

Angela called a greeting in return.

"How'd you know she was there?" he felt driven to ask.

A tiny pause; then Casey said, "She always waits outside for me."

He frowned as Casey walked to her teacher without a sign of awkwardness.

Sam murmured, "It's a security thing. Routine's vital for kids with challenges." She watched her baby with pride in her eyes.

Something about Casey's expertise niggled at

Brett's mind—something intangible, just out of reach. "I've never seen a blind child with such confidence, Sam. It's almost as if she can—can see…just a little?"

"I know." Sam sounded even more strained. "I've thought the same thing a thousand times. Don't do it to her, Brett. I've put her through the tests four times already. Her blindness is profound. All this kind of thinking does is make her think you don't love her as she is. She's more insecure than she seems…"

With a stifled sound, she almost ran into the building housing the pool.

Damn it, Glennon, you're only opening your mouth to change feet. He shook his head with a sigh. Thinking she could see was probably no more than his own stupid wishes for Casey—and look where all his dreams had got them so far.

Casey's swim class held three other kids. They interacted with the familiarity of long friendship, bouncing around on the bench seat, talking about their week.

"I got a father," Casey announced with a touch of pride. "He came here today."

Angela turned to see him and put her hand out, smiling. "Angela Carstairs."

"Brett Glennon." He shook the woman's hand, feeling the sincerity radiate from her.

"I don't have a dad now," a boy beside Casey sighed. "I don't think he liked me."

Casey replied, "I used to think my dad was dead, but he came back. He takes me loads of places. Maybe your dad will do that, too!"

Brett's eyes met Sam's for a brief moment. Hers were aloof. He deserved that, he supposed.

The pool had rails all the way around and Olympic-style rubber dividers all the way down. The kids walked into the pool via the pebbled walkway, chatting and giggling, until Angela called them to order. Then she took turns taking the children in, telling the others to practice their floating while they waited.

"I thought there'd be more teachers—one on one," Brett muttered.

"There used to be." Sam's eyes remained with her daughter. "But government funds have been cut, and benefit nights don't cover everything. There's money for the kids' needs, but this is an optional extra. Besides, these kids can swim now. The other teachers are needed for the high-needs kids in the hydrotherapy pool."

He frowned, looking around at the magnificent

pool and all the equipment for the kids. Everything seemed new and up-to-date. "They don't appear to suffer from lack of funds here."

"We raise half the money ourselves. Phone operators asking for donations, sweepstakes, charity dos, benefit nights, craft stalls, a garden show— we do a lot to keep things afloat."

Brett watched Casey swim with a sense of wonder and deep, haunting guilt. What if Sam or Casey had desperately needed help in the past? Had his wife and daughter been forced to live off charity carelessly given by a stranger in the street while he'd been off saving the world?

"Who uses the hydrotherapy pool on what days, and what for?" he asked, wanting to know more about this amazing place.

"Mostly it's for the kids with multiple disabilities." Sam smiled. "You should see them. These kids can't walk or move very well, but when they're in the warm water, it's like they've found freedom. They can move around on their own, dog-paddling or swimming. It makes them feel almost normal. The smiles on their faces are brighter than diamonds. The happiness they feel keeps us going to raise more funds for new equipment."

"What pieces have you bought lately?" he

asked, fascinated. What did Casey need that Sam couldn't provide? He wanted to do *something* for his daughter…

"We've updated the floor trampoline and bought new gym equipment. Even rolling on a bouncing tramp or over a gym ball stretches the backs and limbs of kids with severe mobility problems and gives them the exercise and stimulation they need, and they love it. They sleep better for the exercise—and the parents get a break. Some of these kids barely sleep at night unless they've had their time at the gym or pool. Knowing you've helped lessen the load of a stressed-out family trying to keep their challenged child at home with them is a wonderful feeling. There's nothing like it."

Sam glowed with the words. She looked vivid, radiant as she talked of the Centre. Never had she been so lovely. The smile on her face, the light in her eyes, showed her passion for her subject. She'd found a new vocation. Serenity and accomplishment shone from her. She looked…contented. Fulfilled. Happy.

Once, that passion and glow was for me. I was her vocation. Making me happy was all she wanted or thought about.

Half-ashamed of the selfish thought—God knows he needed her, but these kids just *needed*—he kept drawing her out. "What sort of things do *you* do to raise funds?"

She grinned. "You'd be surprised at the talents I've picked up." The smile turned sheepish as she added, "I crochet now. I make finger puppets and rugs for the craft stalls. I bake cakes for the markets. I've planted flowers and herbs for the garden show in August. There's a charity auction next week—I took special lessons for that."

"What lessons?"

She grinned. "Come and see if you're still around. You never know, you might feel the urge to donate when you see what's up for sale."

If you're still around.

On those words of unconscious provocation, the take-me-or-leave-me attitude that hurt and intrigued him, she turned to the other three parents, introducing him only as Casey's father.

I'm not a Glennon...

Like a wake-up call, a sudden flurry of cold droplets rained over him. Startled, he yelled, "What the—"

His daughter's goggled, swim-capped, grinning face bobbed up from the edge of the pool. "I do that to Mummy to see if she's watching me. You weren't watching, Brett!"

He laughed, relaxing. "I watched you for ages. You're a really good swimmer, aren't you?"

Casey preened. "Angela says I'm *excellent*."

"She's right. I couldn't swim that well at five."

A young man came over to the side of the pool closest to where Angela taught kicking techniques. After a few words with him, she helped her charge out and addressed the parents. "I've got an important phone call. I'll be back soon. Can you mind the children for a few minutes?"

Though moments before they had been deep in conversation about the upcoming charity auction, the three mothers and one father broke up the circle and turned to focus on their children.

Brett, wading deep through the guilt at what these people had done for his wife and child during his absence, said, "Keep going with your arrangements. I'll play with the kids."

The other parents nodded and smiled. Only Sam hesitated. "The surrounds are nonslip, but the kids are wet... If they—"

Brett laid a finger over her mouth. "Then we'll sit and play. Okay?"

After a long moment, Sam nodded.

He caressed her mouth with a trailing finger until she moved back to the group, her natural lithe grace touched with the tautness of the desire she tried so hard to hide from him.

Was she afraid of him or of what he could do to her with a simple touch? Last night indicated that she was far from neutral to his touch, no matter what she said.

The photos…her response…all told a truth her mouth was unwilling to say—at least in words. When they'd kissed, her mouth *cried* out the truth. She wouldn't be so responsive to him, surely, if there was another man?

All those years since he'd called from Africa and she'd never been home, he'd worried about that one possibility. It seemed for nothing. Sam wasn't a player. If she had another man, she'd have told him—he knew that.

The field was clear, at least in that. She was free to love him, if only he could—

"What'll we play?" a little boy named Mickey asked.

Brett, brought back to the present, thought swiftly. Oh, help. How did people entertain these kids? It seemed everything he could think of to play was taboo: hide and seek, tag, I spy. He was a doctor, for heaven's sake! *Think,* he told himself in desperation.

"How about we sing songs?" he asked in a rush.

"Yeah!" The general consensus left him limp with relief.

"Right. Who knows 'Ring Around the Rosie'? Oops, we can't do that—the floor's wet, and I promised your mums I'd keep you sitting."

The kids laughed at him, calling him a silly man...and he felt like one, the way Casey's lips drooped. He was embarrassing her.

So much for the hero dad maintaining his status without using money.

Desperate to redeem himself, he suggested, "How about 'Pop Goes the Weasel'?"

"That's boring!" The other girl, Kate, protested.

Brett laughed. "Ah, but you haven't tried the special Glennon brand. I'm the weasel!"

Intrigued, the kids demanded to be shown the game.

"Can you all sing the song?"

Dutifully, with a touch of scorn, the kids sang the chorus. Brett shouted in mock horror, "Where's the 'pop'? That was the most pathetic attempt at a pop I ever heard! No weasel worth a scratch is gonna pop for you guys!"

The kids giggled again. "Well, how *do* we 'pop'?" Casey demanded, looking as intrigued as the rest of them, and he drew a silent sigh of relief. Her embarrassment was a thing of the past.

"Right—here goes your first lesson in sound effects." Taking Casey's hand, he lifted her index finger, placing it in her mouth. Then he did the same to the other three. "Okay. Now put your finger against the side of your mouths, near the edge—yeah, the outside there, that's great—and close your mouth around it. Uh-huh. Now hold your breaths…can you do that? All *right!* Now push your finger against your mouth as you pull it out real quick. Go!"

A succession of four tiny pops issued forth from their mouths, followed by delighted giggles. "We did it!" Casey yelled, her pretty face alive with joy.

Brett felt a rush of pride. Casey's pop had been the best! Casey seemed so advanced for her age and disability. He heard a little whisper deep within himself, an echo of that pride. *That's my kid.* If only…

Briskly he got on with the business of improving their pops before he became a weasel. Then he snuck around the group as they sang. When the time for the pop came, he pounced gently on one child, while the others screamed with laughter, although they couldn't see the other's reaction. They knew where he was every time but allowed him to "scare" them and to share in the joke.

They were such happy kids—and unlike most "normal" kids, they gave each other their dignity instead of getting their self-esteem from picking on each other.

As they sang a sitting version of "Ring Around the Rosie," he held Casey's hand and the hand of a kid he didn't know an hour ago, and was unsure of whether he would touch him if he *did* know him—and he felt another strange rush of warmth. The little hand was so trusting...

Casey, to his left, lifted her shining face and smiled right into his eyes—again, almost as if she could see him. He'd *almost* swear she could—

Stop it!

From the loose hold, he turned his hand and twined his fingers through his child's. He smiled back at her as that soft warmth filled his heart again. He was unable to look away for a very long time. Gently he bent forward to kiss the velvet cheek, and Casey's smile softened even more. Man, he was turning into total mush for this beautiful little girl. She already had him wrapped right around her little finger—and right now it felt like the best place in the world to be.

And when he looked up, Sam was watching him interact with his daughter, and her eyes were full of sweet surprise…and the beginnings of real respect.

Angela returned at that moment, and the swimming lesson continued on a limited time frame, as the kids with a greater need for hydrotherapy would come next.

When he approached the other parents, the smiles were warmer, more welcoming than when Sam had introduced him. With the passing of a game, he'd become one of them.

Sam kept talking about the upcoming function. "So how many of us have signed the waiver for the auction? We can't afford to have any legal repercussions for this, so only those who've signed the waiver can be put up for sale."

Brett blinked. *People…?* Then it dawned on him. "You're selling dates with single parents or relatives of the kids?"

One of the other parents, Anne, nodded and smiled. "We've already had advance bids on three of the 'items.'" And she grinned at Sam, who closed her eyes as she blushed. "Five hundred dollars for Sam is our best."

He felt Sam's foot touch his in silent warning. *No one knew Sam was his wife*. And she wanted it to stay that way. But everything inside him rose up in red-hot rebellion. Another man buying the right to have time with *his* wife?

"I officially bid five thousand dollars for a date with Sam."

He'd kept his tone casual, but all four parents gasped and turned to Sam, whose blush now covered her face.

"Whatever the highest bid ends up for Sam, I will double it." He smiled at them all in turn, at the dropped jaws and staring eyes. "Well, all for a good cause, right…our kids."

The grins were back, and he knew he'd made an unforgettable impact.

Sam spoke, making an obvious effort not to talk through gritted teeth. "May I please speak with you, Brett? Alone?"

Bland, smiling, he replied, "Of course, Sam."

She led the way to the opposite end of the pool, taking care to not tread in the wide puddles the kids had caused during the lesson, even though she wore sneakers. Brett wondered if any vestiges of his reckless Sam still existed. If they did, she was hiding them so deep inside herself, nothing showed but the cautious woman he'd seen consistently since the first night of his return.

Except when I kiss her.

On that cheerful thought, he turned Sam around to face him. "I think this is alone enough to say what we need to. I have the right to tell those people I'm more than Casey's dad. And to bid for you. Don't try to tell me I don't."

Expecting an angry retort, he was broadsided by the pain in those lovely eyes. "You have the right to say whatever you want, Brett, but it's me that has to live with the consequences of whatever comes out of your mouth when you're gone again."

He wanted so badly to say, *I'm not going anywhere.* But she wouldn't believe it. "I will not have any man winning a date with you, Sam. You're *my* wife."

"Stop it," she whispered, looking frantic. "Don't talk so loud. If Casey finds out we're married, she's going to start wanting more than I can give her."

"Such as?" He'd be damned if Casey would go without anything from now on. If Sam couldn't afford it—

"Like a united family." The words shocked him. "Like little brothers and sisters and a daddy who lives with us." Her voice was drenched in sadness, killing the words rising to be heard. "I can't guarantee her those things, Brett, and neither can you."

He stared at her. "Guarantee? We're her parents, not a toy or a TV. We aren't appliances. Nobody in life has guarantees of anything, Sam."

She sighed and scrubbed at her eyes. "You don't get it. Casey's an insecure, frightened child. She deserves that security, that happiness—"

"Are you talking about Casey or yourself?" he said right over her. "I know you think that because I had a family and money, I had a perfect existence. Maybe I did, compared to you. But nobody's life is perfect, Sam. If you're teaching her she's been ripped off and deserves more than the rest of the human race because she's blind, you're doing her a real disservice."

She closed her eyes. "I know that compared to the kids in Africa—"

"This isn't about comparisons, Sam—not to kids in Africa or sighted kids, rich kids or *any* kind of kid. It's not about comparing her childhood to yours, either." Grabbing her by the shoulders, he turned her to face the opposite end of the pool where the kids were playing a game of above-water Marco Polo. "Take a good look at her, Sam. Casey's neither insecure nor frightened.

She's a very happy kid who knows she's loved. And she knows, if you don't, that her dad is here to stay. If Casey wants a real family, as far as I'm concerned, she can have it."

Sam whitened so fast, he thought she might pass out where she stood. "No."

She couldn't make her rejection any clearer—and the anguish of shattered hopes sent a shot of pain through him. He needed to get alone, and fast, before he became a bloody wreck in front of her. "Then if Casey asks, *you* tell her who's stopping us becoming a family, Sam."

A soft gasp of shock. "Brett…"

"No." He turned to the door. "I'm tired of being the villain for you. I'm through covering for your insecurities so you can feel better about yourself. I can't even tell my kid that I'm married to her mother." He headed for the door. He had to get out—

"Brett! Brett…"

The one voice guaranteed to halt him in his tracks—and to his startled surprise, it also brought the screaming terror and the pain to a sudden halt. His mind filled with Casey, with her acceptance of him and her sweetness, and banished the darkness inside. "Hey, kiddo."

Casey was dripping wet, with her hands reaching out for the towel she'd hung on a hook on the wall beside the pool. "Wanna see the rest of the Centre? I can show you…"

Another surprise. Her cute self-importance made him laugh and filled the empty spaces inside him with warmth and light. "I'd love to."

"I'll be dressed in a minute. Wait for me!" She turned for the dressing rooms.

"Brett, please…"

He turned to face Sam, but even the white face, the pleading eyes couldn't move him; there was too much at stake. "So I don't have the right to bid on a date with you, and I don't have the right to tell my daughter the truth on an issue that could destroy *my* relationship with her for the rest of our lives? If I leave for Melbourne to visit my sick parents and you disappear again while I'm gone, are you going to lie to her about where I went, and why, so that you can keep her to yourself?" His eyes burned into hers. "What did I do to earn this distrust, but go where I'd given my word to be before we met—and get taken against my will?"

"Sam, we have a question about the dinner— oh, sorry, we can wait…"

Sam opened her eyes and forced a smile. "No,

Anne, it's fine." She glanced at Brett. "Can you take Casey for a little while? I can find you later."

As the beginnings of trust, it was tentative, fragile even, but it was a step forward. *A baby step.* She was offering a tiny olive branch, and he'd be a proud fool to not take it. He hesitated. "I'll meet you at the car in an hour or so."

She nodded. "Brett…" Her hand touched his softly. "I wish… If I could make you…"

He held his breath, waiting. But then she was gone without warning.

The unseen war continued, the ghosts that haunted them both keeping them apart.

Casey showed him around the Centre. He learned how the difference in path sounds and textures showed the children where they were, rather than simple signs in Braille. He followed her in awe as Casey led with complete confidence through the winding paths to a pretty garden area in its middle, where the path led downward from concrete to Pebblecrete to dirt to planks.

Casey was such a smart girl, so sweet and clever and brave and beautiful. *If only I were a good enough surgeon to cure her…*

"This is the middle of the Centre, Brett. Wanna ride?"

He looked around with a half smile of memory. He'd seen this place on television a while back when Angry Anderson—a hard-rock singer now less famous for his bad-boy ways than his determination to help—had raised the funds for this park and built it in a weekend. Built with the needs of the children here in view, it had three different types of paths, swings with seat belts and a monorail for two, so that a minder could ride with a child who could not sit up alone. All the rides, as well as a little garden seat, were set in a bower covered in wisteria vines and trailing flowers. Every ride had handles, belts and safety precautions, so that any child here could enjoy its benefits.

It was…beautiful, haunting. Just a little train park, but for these kids it meant freedom, especially for kids with multiple disabilities.

"I'd love to." He took a moment to learn how to strap them both in, and then they took the little train ride a hundred feet to the other side of the park. They swung and slid down the dip.

From a quiet corner of the garden, Sam stood in silence and watched father and daughter start to bond with a mixture of pride, concern, fear and deep, abiding love. She ached to join them on that little train and complete the circle.

As much as she ached to snatch Casey in her arms and run until he couldn't find them. But it was too late. Her baby's heart was going to be broken sooner or later. Her contentment with what her mother could provide was gone. From now on, Casey would always want more—time, attention, fun and games and material things—than Sam would ever be able to provide.

Brett hadn't changed in essentials. He'd always sought perfection and believed you only had to reach hard and high enough to find it. He reached for the stars, hung on to his dreams with a death grip. And now Casey had touched the stars, felt them with her fingertips, would she ever be able to let go? And God help her if Brett infused Casey with the hope he'd mentioned today. The surgeon, the dreamer who wanted to cure the world, wanted to heal his daughter's dead optic nerve. If he said a word of his dream when Casey was in his hearing…

Brett had never known the meaning of *failure*— but in his daughter's obvious imperfection, he was about to learn. At the cost of a tiny girl's broken heart.

CHAPTER SEVEN

"HEY, BRETT, YOU WANNA come home for dinner?"

Sam's insides clenched at the innocent question, the half-hopeful look on Casey's sweet face as she delivered the invitation—and the way she'd unconsciously picked up on Brett's way of saying "hey" before asking a question.

Dear God, how life repeats. From mother to daughter, the instant and irresistible fascination for Brett Glennon continued.

She felt Brett's eyes on her for a brief instant before he replied in a tone whose gravity belied the wicked light dancing in his eyes, "Who could resist an invitation from an angel?"

Casey bounced around beneath her seat belt, excited at the prospect of spending more time with this amazing, fun person she could claim as her father. All the kids had liked him today, and he hadn't given them a single thing except the gift of dignity and liking them as they were.

Sam kept her eyes trained out the window during the five-minute trip from the Centre to home. She didn't need to see his face to feel the triumph inside him. He thought he was so close to winning. She could almost hear his thought: *Casey likes me—me, not what I gave her.*

He still didn't realise that wasn't the issue. As far as she was concerned, Shakespeare's wisdom was bunkum. She'd rather Casey had never loved her father at all than loved and lost him. Though she'd never wish Casey to be as fatherless as she'd been, Sam knew too well the devastation of loving and losing Brett—and now she had no choice but to allow Casey to go through that. She couldn't believe he'd stay with them, no matter how many promises he made that he'd always be around. Brett made the world a more exciting place—and more dangerous. She just wanted her little girl to stay safe...

Which little girl—little Casey or little Sam?

She sighed. She'd learned from bitter experience that Brett's forever promises were like the flame of fire, easily felt, warming the soul, but quickly doused when a new opportunity to save the world came his way. Brett was true hero material, his invisible wings set to soar to the sky—and through no fault of their own, she and Casey were forever chained to the ground.

He was Casey's hero now. Sam knew her sightless eyes watched him soaring. She was flying vicariously beneath his wings—and she'd always want to keep trying to fly beside him with wings that would be forever clipped.

Brett gave her a quick glance, his brow furrowed, obviously misinterpreting her silence. "Sam? Is my staying a problem financially? I'll order takeout."

"No, thanks," she sighed. "I think Casey's had enough takeout in the past two days."

Casey grumbled to herself.

"I've got stuff for pizza," Sam consoled her, feeling hurt.

"Okay," Casey agreed, but she sounded glum. "Can me 'n' Brett go get cola? I can sit in the front seat with Brett…"

"Sounds good, kiddo," Brett put in before Sam could open her mouth.

"Lemonade, please," Sam told Brett. "She's had enough caffeine the past two days to make her hyper for a week."

Brett nodded with a long-suffering grin that

turned her insides to mush. "I'll get used to the routine in time."

She closed her mouth before she could blurt out *Is that a promise or a threat?*

"I *like* this car," Casey announced with a sigh, smoothing her hand over the soft leather interior. "Can we get one? It's *much* nicer than catchin' smelly buses 'n' trains all the time!"

Sam gritted her teeth, aching for all the things she could never give Casey. "Sorry, princess. You'll just have to wait for Brett's visits for the car rides." She leaped out of the opulent four-wheel-drive as soon as Brett pulled up in the driveway. "Hop in the front, Casey. Go get the lemonade, and I'll make pizza." She looked at Brett. "There's a store just around the corner." She flew to the door and into the kitchen, taking out pizza ingredients, making pizzas and dashing at her eyes every few seconds. It wasn't the day, it was the onions…

"Is there anything I can do?" Brett put down the bottle of soft drink and a chocolate dessert on the counter, his eyes telling her he could sense her disquiet.

Sam, worn out with the turmoil in her heart, said bluntly, "Yes. You can take your money, your fancy car, your takeaway food and your I-am-rich-and-can-give-you-what-you-like popularity back to Melbourne and leave Casey and me in what peace we can find once you're gone."

"Sam." The quietness of the rebuke in no way hid Brett's hurt.

"We were happy," she muttered, chopping the onion and peppers for the pizza with savage intent. "We were doing fine. Then you come and turned us upside down. Casey never knew about skating or fast food or pizza restaurants or traveling everywhere in luxury cars before you—and she liked the bus and train. Now it will take me months—maybe even years—to settle her down to our normal lives."

"Damn it, Sam, it's not as if she has to settle down to anything! I can support her—" His harsh tone faltered as he twisted Sam around, seeing the devastation in her eyes, the tracks of tears on her cheeks. His face softened. "It's been damn hard for you the past six years, hasn't it? I've disrupted more than your routine, haven't I?"

Feeling too tired to argue, she nodded.

He held her shoulders, his fingers soothing, arousing her. "What do you want me to do?"

"Go in to Casey. Have fun." She looked up.

"But don't play the divorced daddy, spoiling her to make her love you. Daddies aren't just pizza providers. Any deadbeat dad can show up, give presents and fun and disappear. But real fathers are here for the long haul. And special-needs kids are just that. Their needs never end. If you make her love you, she'll need you, too—and if you don't stay, she'll never forget, never stop hurting or wishing. I know."

He seemed at a loss. After a long moment, his hands on her shoulders and his eyes fixed on the wall behind her, he asked again, "What do I do?"

Sam frowned. "You really don't know, do you?" she asked slowly, almost in wonder. "You're a doctor. You tell others about their responsibilities, what patients need."

He shrugged, blowing out a sigh. "For the first time, I've realised how easy that is. Diagnosis, prescribing medications and giving advice that's no more than theory—for me, at least. I can send them home to their families, who do the hard work. This is the life I come home to. This is my kid." He shook his head. "Help me, Sam. I want to do this right."

Sam turned back to the meal, unnerved with this new, vulnerable Brett. "Read to her. Put on a tape, dance and sing with her. Talk to her. Get to know her, as you did today."

Turning her around with his hands, he looked deeply into her eyes. For the first time, there was no argument, no rejection. Her heart pounding and her legs like jelly, Sam smiled at him. When he dipped his head to hers, she didn't step away, didn't turn her face or speak a word, but, *aching* for his touch, the kiss that made her feel so…so… She met him halfway.

Again he surprised her. His lips, soft and warm, grazed her cheek. "Tell me if I'm making things harder for you, Sam. I want to help you, not upset you. I'm here for you—always."

Through the lump in her throat, her voice was only a strangled whisper. "Don't, Brett…"

"I know I let you down when you needed me most. I was so damned focused on my dreams I ignored your needs, your hopes and fears—and your body's changes. I could have—*should* have—seen your pregnancy, but I remained wilfully blind to it. I won't do that again, Sam," he whispered, holding her. "From here on in, I will always be there for you. For the rest of our lives. I'll never leave you alone again."

Sam sighed, resting her cheek on Brett's chest

for a brief, sweet moment, and wished that she could believe.

In the shadows of the doorway, a little girl who'd asked her father to spend an evening with her heard him whisper his love to her mother, heard the love in his voice as he held her. She bit her lip and turned away, returning to the empty living room alone.

"…so Greg the Goose touched down at Maisie and Michael's house—feel that, kiddo? Yeah, that's *house*—and they fell asleep. And when they awoke, they decided to tell nobody—not even their mum and dad—of their adventure. For after all, who would believe it? They hardly believed it themselves!" Brett closed the book. "Not a bad story, hey, kid?"

"It was very nice. Thank you, Brett."

Sam saw Brett sigh at the third polite, stilted set of thanks Casey had given him tonight. She watched as he gave a swift glance toward the little-used secondhand TV, seeming to wish he could relegate this stubborn child to it so he could continue wooing her mother.

The magic between father and daughter had flitted to oblivion, along with the sparkle in

Casey's eyes and the laughter in her voice, leaving Brett angry and frustrated, so unused to losing with any female. But Casey wasn't just any female. She was his flesh and blood, sitting facing him like a tiny mirror image, arms crossed tightly and a mutinous frown on her face.

Casey had declared war on Brett's attempts to get closer...and she wasn't budging an inch.

But Sam felt no urge to laugh. If Brett had an unexpected battle on his hands that he didn't know how to win, it was the kind of painful loss Sam knew and understood far more than Brett ever would. Casey couldn't see him, so his good looks and rakish smile were wasted on her. And he'd agreed not to use his wealth to influence Casey to his side. But it was obvious he wanted his daughter to love him, and Casey had retreated behind barricades he didn't know how to cross.

A catch-22 situation rich in irony; a Glennon who couldn't get what he wanted within twenty-four hours must be a life-altering situation for Brett. He was facing the one female he couldn't charm with good looks, his wealth or famous charm or even his love—because Casey was a Glennon, too. She'd inherited Brett's stubbornness, the will to win against a worthy opponent.

If David Glennon could see his mutinous granddaughter holding up a wall of stubborn pride that her own father couldn't beat down, he'd be proud of her. Casey was a Glennon, all right. She took after the old fox more than Sam had envisioned in her worst nightmares.

As soon as the dishes were done, Sam hustled Casey into bed. Casey said good night to Brett with the same cool reserve she'd given him the night they met. No mock-solemn handshakes, no flash of dimples, no asking when he'd be back—this time.

Perhaps Casey thought she knew the answer.

Knowing her daughter, Sam understood. Little Miss Big Ears had come in to hear what was going on and was now suffering the proverbial pain of the eavesdropper.

Even if he knew, Brett couldn't possibly understand how much he'd hurt her.

"I've made hot chocolate," she said quietly when she entered the lounge.

He balled his fists into his pockets. "What happened to her, Sam? One minute she was my best friend, the next, I'm a stranger again."

Sam sighed. "She's a kid, Brett, and the usual weather vane with her likes and dislikes. Maybe she's noticed that you rarely call her by her name unless you're frustrated. It's pretty distancing being called 'kid'—it's as if you've forgotten her name."

A brow lifted; he looked at her in open cynicism. "I know my own daughter's name, even if I didn't have the chance to participate in her naming."

"Or it could be that you gave up so quickly," she went on, leading up to the real truth with caution; he had to be ready to hear it—and if Casey was listening in, she might be even more hurt by his first reaction. "Within twenty minutes you wanted to relegate her to the TV."

Brett shrugged, infuriating her. "All men get tired at the end of a long day, Sam."

"That's an excuse—"

His eyes blazed. "And you're an expert on how fathers react with their kids? Which of your four fantastic foster fathers was so great, you can compare me so badly against them?"

Sam closed her mouth, refusing to reply to the harsh words. If she was honest, she knew he was right. She had no idea how fathers behaved with their children. Maybe her ideas for fatherhood were fairy tales she'd idealised from books, Mike Brady and Ward Cleaver, wishing more for Casey than she'd had for herself. Maybe the hurting child inside her expected perfection from Brett, both as father and husband, which had her continually finding fault with him.

She'd once wanted a fairy-tale prince—and she'd had him, all too briefly. It hurt too much to have dreams come true when they didn't last.

It seemed Brett wasn't the only perfectionist in this broken family.

"Maybe you're right. I *don't* know what a loving father would do," she admitted with the sadness of looking into an emotional mirror and feeling ashamed by what she saw there.

Brett sighed. "If I gave you an excuse, Sam, it's one I've been giving myself for years as the reason why my father never spent time with me. Dad was much better when I became a teenager, someone he could talk to." Brett's fingers wafted over her cheek. "Give me time, Sam. I don't know how to be a father yet, but I'm trying."

"Try calling her Casey," she whispered, feeling the gentle stirrings of need for touch—*his* touch—in her deepest soul.

"You're the expert." Lips followed fingers, a butterfly caress. "Anything you say, boss."

His smiling lips met hers. Sam couldn't hold out. She melted into him, hands holding his shoul-

ders as a lifeline. He lifted her up into his arms
and seduced her heart with a kiss filled with tenderness, filling her with memories of the love that,
for her, hadn't died, couldn't ever seem to die.

"Sam, oh, Sam," he whispered against her lips,
every breath a sweet rush of warm coffee-laced
chocolate, drowning her senses with sweetness.
"I've made mistakes, but I've paid the price for
losing you. I feel like I've been paying the price
every day for six damned long, lonely years. Let
me in, Sam. I need you so damned much."

And through the mists of sensual delight surrounding her, through the need for his loving that
was like a knife piercing her, she dimly compre-
hended his meaning.

She had to fight her own emotions here. There
was more at stake than her needs alone. She
would never allow Brett to win when it meant
Casey could suffer the inevitable rejection
awaiting her in a father who'd never had to learn
how to lower his expectations.

Within two days he'd stated his intention for
her, Casey's mother, several times. But he'd said
nothing about Casey herself—and Casey must,
must come first.

Using her hands, she pushed back against his

shoulders, trying to find some space between their bodies, to gain distance and perspective. "This can't happen, Brett."

"But it's going to," he whispered, his eyes black with passion. "I promise you it will."

Sam gulped down the pain filling her throat and shook her head. "No. I told you—Casey will always come first with me. You will get nothing from me until Casey knows she can trust you to always be there for her."

The smile with his whispered promise had faded with her first words. "If you want an ironclad contract that I'm here for good, Sam—"

"Not for me, Brett—for Casey. And," she went on with gentle remorselessness, "I suppose I need that, too. I no longer trust you to stay, Brett. I don't believe you want *us* for longer than it would take to complete your own healing. I can't believe you're not planning to return to Africa or some other needing place as soon as your leg is healed."

He put her back on her feet. "You really have changed," he said, his voice jerky. "Time was once, if I had you at that level of passion, nothing else mattered."

She met his eyes. *Fight for Casey's sake*. "That didn't answer my question."

A muscle jerked at the side of his mouth. "Nobody can give guarantees to stay forever, Sam. You could die tomorrow."

She lost patience then. "Don't argue semantics, Brett. Are you going back to Africa?" *And leaving us behind again? Are you going to break my little girl's heart...and mine?*

"No, I'm not." The words were curt with agony tight-leashed. "I'll never go back. I don't need to. It never leaves me, not for a damned day."

About to press on with her own fears and needs, his words—and the naked suffering etched on his face—stopped her dead. Until now she'd only thought of how Brett was never here when she needed him most. But as she'd said last night, abandonment went both ways.

And he was still paying the price.

Why had she never noticed the lines of pain, the anguish held inside his tight voice? Casey had seen it the first night...and Sam had ignored every sign.

"I'm sorry." She pressed her lips together. "I...didn't see...what you've been through."

After a long moment, which seemed to last far longer, he nodded but didn't speak.

"You're planning to make us all go back,

aren't you?" she asked very softly. "To Melbourne, I mean."

The cane clattered to the floor as he lifted his hands, slowly clenching into fists before they fell. "I...don't...know. All I know is I need you, Sam. I need Casey. I came here because I needed a family, normality. I have to end this damn nightmare somehow!"

The growl was filled with pain, both physical and emotional, and she longed to hold him close and kiss him until it subsided...but she dared not. He was standing alone, *so alone,* and he needed to speak, not to have his mouth closed by her clumsy attempts at comfort. This was a Brett she didn't understand, but she *needed* to know this side of him, for his sake.

"The way my life is now, it's all I can do to manage getting through one damned day at a time. Right now I'm trying to not fall down like a stupid drunk at your feet—but here I am, fighting to stay upright so you'll tell me what I did wrong to turn my daughter into a block of ice tonight and you back into the overprotective lioness ready to tear me apart."

His knee gave way as he finished; he had to hang on to the back of a chair to stay upright.

All Sam's beliefs about having his choices forced upon her, her smug notions of right and wrong, even her need to punish him, withered and died in a moment.

If Brett had killed *her* dreams by leaving for Africa, it seemed Brett's had turned into a never-ending nightmare—and for far deeper reasons than his shattered knee alone. His edited version of how he'd received his knee injury was telling enough. And yet she'd ignored his need for healing, pandering to her fears by focusing on what Casey wanted and needed. Putting herself and Casey first, despite all signs that the man she'd vowed to care for in sickness and in health was in desperate need of that care.

She hadn't realised how isolated and self-centred she'd become. In trying to make the world safe for Casey—and if she was honest, for herself—she'd locked out the rest of the world...including Casey's father, who was doing his damnedest to open the door, to maybe find some safety and some healing inside, where he belonged.

Or where he ought to belong—if she hadn't locked him out. Wanting guarantees, wanting *safety*. He was taking all the chances here, and she was being nothing but a damned coward.

She bent to pick up his cane and handed it to him. When he leaned on it, his eyes softening with relief from physical stress, she reached out, almost trembling with fear, to touch his cheek. "Do you have painkillers somewhere?"

His eyes closed. He moved his face against her hand as if he was as starved for touch as she was. "In my jacket pocket."

"Lie down on the chaise." She found his jacket tossed on a sofa, found the pills and ran for water. When she came back, he was still lowering himself onto the chaise, his face stiff and pale. She let him get settled—too well she knew how he'd feel if she tried to help—and held out the glass and two tablets, as prescribed on the bottle.

"Just one," he said through gritted teeth. "Otherwise I won't get off this thing tonight."

"Then stay," she said quietly. When he looked up at her, his face white and strained, she smiled gently. "You shouldn't drive back to the hotel in this condition."

He nodded and swallowed the water and pills. "Thank you."

So awkward, so stilted and polite. A thin film

of cold—of *fear*—lay over all they said and did. "I'm sorry I've been so hard on you. I was protecting—"

"No. I came…barging into your life without warning, trailing my mess behind me, expecting too much." He spoke so softly, she had to close her eyes to concentrate. "I expected you to fit in with my plans, my life, just like you did before— to make my life better." He sighed and closed his eyes. "But I don't know you anymore, Sam, and I hate that. I hate it."

The lump in her throat *hurt*. "I had no choice, Brett."

He gave her a weary smile. "I understand that. Believe me, I know. I know we can't go back to the way we were…*I* can't go back. I just wish I knew where to go from here, because I won't give up on us without…one hell of a fight."

She crouched beside the chaise and told him the truth. "Casey heard what you said in the kitchen, that you'd always be there for me—for *me*. You never mentioned her. She thought you'd come here as her special friend. You shattered her illusions and hurt her."

A whispering sigh touched her skin as his head slowly fell to meet hers, forehead touching forehead. "Oh, man, that was dumb. You told me she listens in on conversations, and I forgot. I'm sorry, Sam, I'm so damned sorry. I would never hurt Casey."

"Don't tell me—tell Casey."

Brett nodded against her forehead, then reached for his cane.

"No," she said quickly. "Wait for the morning, Brett. She's not going anywhere."

He was even paler than before he'd taken the tablets, but he managed a grin. "She's your daughter, Sam. If I don't do it tonight, she won't believe me tomorrow."

She grinned back in rueful acknowledgement of the truth in his words, and he held out his hand for the cane. With slow, heavy steps, every movement showing the massive effort he made, he walked into Casey's room. Half against her will, Sam followed.

Brett stopped at the door. "Casey? Are you awake?"

Casey's voice was a little muffled. Sam knew she'd been crying. "Yes."

"May I come in?" When Casey nodded, Brett limped in a few steps. When he spoke, his voice was strained. "Casey, I'm sorry. I hurt your feelings tonight and I didn't mean to. Because I was speaking to Mummy at the time, I talked about how I feel about her. I didn't mean for you to think you weren't included in those feelings." He hesitated. "We haven't known each other long, but you're my daughter. I'd fight the world to keep you safe and happy. You're part of my life now, and that's forever."

The silence wasn't long, but Sam knew her daughter, and her stomach clenched, waiting for the words to follow. Brett was in for an emotional lambasting, and he was in no state for it.

"You're nice to Mummy. You *talk* to her." The accusation was half hidden in the pillow; she had the sheet pulled up over most of her face, as well.

"And I'm not nice to you?" he asked, his voice level, without defensiveness. Despite the agony he was in, he was open and listening to her.

"No." Casey sounded mutinous. "You didn't tell me why I don't got the same name as you. You didn't tell me why you're sad and how your leg got sore and why you use the stick thing."

"I see." Brett sounded thoughtful now. "I'm sorry. I treated you like you were a little kid, didn't I?"

No answer.

"Can you forgive me? I haven't been a dad for

long—I mean, I haven't known you for long. I'll probably make a lot of mistakes. But I won't know they're mistakes unless you tell me."

Finally Casey's face emerged from the tent she'd made of her pillow and sheet. "Jeb said you prob'ly had other kids…"

"Nope," Brett replied gravely. "You're it so far. I'm still married to your mummy, Casey, so I can't go around having kids anywhere else, can I?"

"Then my name's Glennon, too?" she asked slowly, and Sam gulped. The truth had to come now—Brett couldn't change that any more than she could.

"Yes, Casey, it is. Don't be cranky with Mummy—you see, she was told I'd been killed. She was so sad, she changed her name, wanting to forget everything that hurt her."

"Okay."

Sam drew in a breath of relief. Brett had said exactly the right thing. She wanted to kiss him again for that.

"I'd like a brother or sister to play with. Now you're back, can I have one?"

The provocative little statement was a challenge: either answer her or be locked out again. And Sam had no idea how he'd answer.

"Give me time, Casey," he said, laughing. "The way my leg is now, I'm tired out playing with you. I couldn't catch up with a baby."

"What happened to your leg?" Casey asked, and Sam heaved a tiny sigh of relief. He'd stepped past that emotional land mine to safety.

"Can I sit down? My leg's hurting right now. I only had my last operation on my knee a little while ago, so when I do a lot during the day, it gets pretty sore."

Casey scooted over and left the covers open. "You can lie down if you want."

Realising the olive branch his daughter extended, Brett took up the invitation, lying beside her with a sigh of relief. "Thanks. I might fall asleep while I'm talking, but it won't be on purpose—I just took stuff for the pain. Okay?"

Casey nodded, her face solemn. "Okay."

Brett sighed again. "Have you ever heard of Africa? Of course you have—silly me. Well, I was trying to help people in a place called Mbuka. Some bad men needed a doctor…"

Casey snuggled up to her father, her sightless eyes, trained on the spot from where his voice came, soft and sweet and…and *trusting*.

Sam swiped at tears and walked out to wash the

cups. But she didn't know if she cried for what she couldn't change or for the man who was causing the metamorphosis in her life.

Twenty minutes later, Casey came tiptoeing out of her room. "Mummy, he's crying in his sleep," she whispered. "He's talking about people who punched him and kicked him so he was real sore. Help him, Mummy." She grabbed Sam by the hand and tugged her to her bedroom door, and pushed it open.

It took Sam almost a minute to control the tears stinging her eyes, and the sharp lump in her throat. He looked so *big* in the child's bed, strong and dangerous and yet vulnerable beneath the Cinderella-print light pink sheets. He thrashed around the bed, mumbling garbled words.

Her heart and throat and chest ached, ached for *him*, for all he'd been through alone, and still went through alone: a soldier in a war only he knew. Trembling, she ran her hand through his hair. "Ssshhh. It's all right. You're home now," she whispered awkwardly, expecting no response— but he quieted within moments. "Sam…Sam…"

"I'm here." She caressed his hair over and over, until she knew he slept. Then, like a marionette whose wire has been pulled, she bent and brushed her lips against his cheek. "Sleep well," she whispered, and ran out of the room on noiseless feet, closing the door behind her.

CHAPTER EIGHT

SAM AWOKE AFTER NINE the next morning.

Brett still slept. She and Casey had been creeping around all morning, trying to give him the rest he needed. He'd woken Sam in the night with a dream she dared not wake him from—he'd thrashed around, muttering words she couldn't decipher, but one thing had come through clearly.

Sam, Sam, where are you?

She'd sat beside him, whispering reassurance, holding his hand and keeping his damaged knee as still as possible, helpless until he let her in. But his need was as obvious as the anguish that hadn't left after two years home and safe.

Brett wandered out of Casey's room soon after ten, yawning. "Sorry. Taking two pills helps me catch up on sleep."

She smiled at him and pushed a mug of coffee over the counter. "I think you needed it."

He shrugged, looking uncomfortable. "Did I talk in my sleep?"

"Yes," she said softly. "You did."

Looking frustrated, he looked out the window to where Casey was playing by herself. "When will she get a guide dog?"

"When she's eight. She's still frightened of dogs now, and we decided not to push her."

"That sounds good," he said but sounded vague, his mind on something else. "Sam, I want to tell—"

"I think it's time we talked—"

Brett grinned at her, and her insides turned to mush, all warm and gooey. "Can you get a sitter for Casey tonight? It's time we communicated without worrying about little pitchers."

A date. She hadn't been on a date in six years. Hadn't felt like a *woman* in six years. She smiled back, feeling shaky inside. "There's a few sitters trained to kids' special needs attached to the Centre."

"Get one for tonight if you can." His hand gently touched, then ran up her arm. "I'll foot the bill." He cupped her cheek with his hand, and she felt something pooling into a warm puddle deep inside her. "I'm footing the bills for my daughter from now on, Sam. She'll never want for anything…and you'll never sacrifice your needs to make sure Casey has her needs met."

Pride didn't occur to her. The simple beauty of shedding a burden too long carried alone made her sigh. "Thank you," she said simply. "I'll see if a sitter's available."

"I'll go see to our picnic." He smiled again and went outside, speaking briefly to Casey before he headed out in the car.

He returned an hour later, wearing board shorts and a T-shirt, carrying a picnic basket. "Watch out, folks—Yogi Bear himself would drool over this pic-a-nic basket!"

But Sam was already drooling—and not over the basket. He looked incredible. The dark, cropped locks were starting to curl over his ears. His T-shirt stretched over his lithe chest and flat stomach. And the long shorts dropped over his damaged knee but were short enough to reveal long, muscular legs and hugged the curve of his butt. And instead of his wicked rogue's grin, his warm, gentle smile for Casey was touching. His mischievous golden-brown eyes looked…tender.

And she was fantasising again about what she

couldn't have. *It's Casey's time with her father. It should be nothing to do with me.*

But her heart and body weren't listening to good sense. They wanted and craved, and she could only turn away, praying for strength. He was like the rich Swiss chocolate she couldn't afford to buy.

If she was this bad already, tonight would be exquisite temptation.

In frustrated silence, she led him out to the back veranda where she'd laid out a blanket.

Was this kismet, karma or just plain hormones? Love was such a fickle emotion. The few men she'd met that might have made her happy and been wonderful fathers for Casey had never even reached first base; she knew kissing them would have been like kissing the brother she'd never had. Yet Brett made her forget her name, what day it was. And what was best for her child flew straight out the window.

The fight was on again today. Fighting against Brett, against her raging hormones. Against the needs of her very heart.

"Hey, Casey-girl!" he called across the garden to the flower-covered gazebo-style arbour where his daughter played. "Are you ready for the most dis-*gust*-ing picnic of your entire life?"

Intrigued, Casey demanded, "What's in it?"

Brett laughed. "That's for me to know, you to come and find out!"

Casey came to him along the perfectly set path, her face filled with anticipation.

He opened the basket when she reached him. "Check it out."

Feeling and sniffing her way through the basket, Casey's little face was soon aglow. "Chocolate cake...fried chicken and fries with gravy!"

Sam groaned to herself. Brett and chocolate— what a lethal combination.

A fleeting look of suspicion crossed Cassy's angelic features. "Where's the salad?"

"What salad?" Brett tackled her to the ground, tickling until she shrieked with laughter. "We're Glennons, not rabbits! Glennons don't eat dis-*gust*-ing salad!"

Sam slipped inside the house with a tiny smile on her face. She couldn't be angry with Brett. Swimming against the tide was stupid, and too exhausting to keep up for long.

When she returned, Brett had set up the pool and paraphernalia of floating toys that cocooned Casey, giving her the comforting feeling blind children love. He'd stripped off his T-shirt, and was limping toward the pool. "I'm coming in, Casey-girl!" He climbed slowly down the stairs, wading through the toys to reach her.

He knew Casey needed to be surrounded and approached slowly. He'd taken the trouble to discover blind children's needs. Sam swallowed yet another lump in her throat. How hard it must have been for Brett the past two years, going through physical therapy and operations, waiting, waiting for news of his wife and daughter, and yet still he'd found time to discover Casey's needs, and how to implement them....

She watched, touched beyond words as she watched father and daughter play—he suggested a game of hide-and-seek, Glennon-style, not calling it Blind Man's Bluff. Since Casey had far better listening skills, she beat him hands down.

After the game ended he opened the enormous picnic basket again, and allowed Casey to rummage through it to her heart's content.

After they'd finished playing and Casey was busy rummaging through the picnic baskets, Sam tapped his arm. "Thank you," she whispered, smiling warmly. "That was wonderful."

Brett grinned, nodded and turned his attention back to Casey. And instead of feeling lost at being left out, Sam felt all warm and fuzzy. The father-daughter relationship Sam had missed out on was making Casey glow so bright.

She could relate to that. All through her childhood, she'd never stopped wishing for her mummy or daddy to come and claim her. One parent would have answered her dreams; but Casey, having total security with one parent, naturally wanted to know the other.

Within ten minutes of finishing the rabidly unhealthy lunch—a time filled with silly jokes and general laughter—Casey wanted to swim again.

Brett put his hand up as Sam opened her mouth. "Three things first, Casey-girl." He touched her nose. "One—more zinc on your nose."

Casey groaned. "You sound like Mummy."

"Mummy's right. And keep your hat on. You're turning pink under your hair."

Casey sighed.

Brett grinned. "Two—we wait twenty minutes before we go back in."

"Aw, Brett—!"

"It's all right for you, you can swim so well," he said with a sigh. "But I've got a bad leg, remember, Case? I have to be careful, you know."

"Oh!" Casey sounded as if she'd made a new

discovery—and perhaps she had: ordinary people had limitations, as well. "Okay, then."

"And now for the biggest 'aw' of the lot—we help Mummy pack up the picnic first."

"Oh, no, Brett! Let Mummy do it!"

"Casey." The sound of her name being spoken with such sternness for the first time startled the child. "You're five years old. It's time you learned to do things for yourself."

"I do!" Casey protested. "Michelle makes Mummy tell me to take my plate to the sink, and I make my bed and everything!"

"Michelle's from the Homestart programme at the Centre," Sam explained, feeling awkward at seeing Brett disciplining the child who had up until the past few days been totally her own to teach and guide. "She's teaching Casey to become as independent as possible."

"Good," Brett said. "But it's time she realised her Mummy needs help—and you're going to learn to help," he added sternly to Casey.

Sam was stunned. "But, Brett, she can't possibly—"

He turned on her, his face fierce. "How do you know? How does Casey know?"

Goaded, she retorted, "How do *you* know?"

"I've spent four hours twice a week for the past six months with a teacher from the Royal Blind Society in Melbourne," he replied, stunning her again. "I wanted to find out as much about what Casey needs to do as I could."

Sam's mouth dropped open. "So that's where you learned Braille? And the right techniques for counting and swimming methods?"

He nodded. "And it's where I learned that Casey needs to learn to help out and think of others." Brett hauled Casey to her feet. "Right, Miss Glennon, up you get."

"Am I a Glennon?" Casey interrupted, sounding awed. "Is that my name now?"

"It always was, Casey-girl. You're a Glennon, now and forever. You're my firstborn child. So, Miss Glennon, you can take these cups in and put them on the bench near the sink. And when we've finished helping, we'll play whatever you want." He added, looking at her mutinous face, "C'mon, Casey, show me you can do it!"

Casey's eyes lit with determination as she grasped the cups Brett put into her hand. She felt the area around her feet with her toes, located the path and followed it to the stairs.

Sam planted herself in Brett's path as he

moved to follow Casey. "You're crossing the line," she hissed. "A few months of theory in the Blind Society gives you the right to take over my daughter's discipline and undermine my methods?"

A brow lifted, and she knew he'd picked up this gauntlet before she'd even thrown it down. "Your excessive coddling of her, you mean."

Sam gasped, her mind whirling. "Have you considered how she'll feel if she drops them all and can't locate them?"

"She'll learn about failure. Her blindness doesn't disqualify her from the human race, Sam. She has to learn to fall and pick herself up, just like the rest of us."

Fuming, thwarted by the good sense of his words running smack against her insecurities, she took up the other issue. "You had no right to change her name without consulting me. You're going to confuse her, thinking you're going to stay and be here with her the rest of her life—"

A crash from the kitchen punctuated her last word.

Brett held Sam back. "I started this; I'll fix it." He led the way in. "But think of this—*I'm* not the one who changed her right and legal name—you did. And I still don't know why." He stalked into the house. "Hey, Case, did you break anything?"

Sam rushed into the house. "Don't ask her that! The only way she can check is with her hands— Casey, sweetie, don't touch anything—" She bolted past Brett into the kitchen.

Casey stood still in the centre of the kitchen amid a semirainbow of fallen picnic crockery, her hands upward, arms extended as if distancing herself from the minidisaster. "I—I dropped everything, Brett," Casey wailed, her lower lip protruding.

Sam ran forward, but again Brett held her back with a hand on her shoulder. "My mess," he mouthed. "What—*everything*? Now, how on earth did you—"A loud crash completed his mock tirade as he dropped his own collection of colourful picnicware.

"Oops," Brett said, sounding guilty and frightened.

Casey gasped, distracted from her own problem. "Did you drop *everything,* Brett?"

"Everything," he assured her solemnly.

Casey giggled, her fear vanishing.

Brett leaned into her, whispering his next words. "Tell you what, Case, how about we get this cleaned up before Mummy comes in?"

Casey giggled, pushing him away playfully. "Mummy's here already."

Brett stilled. His eyes blazed with sudden eagerness, and Sam knew he was thinking again the words he'd said yesterday: *It's as if she can see.* "How do you know?"

"I—I know her smell. I can hear her breathing."

Sam gazed at her daughter, a deep frown between her brows. Casey looked so normal standing there, laughing with Brett over her crashed plates, and part of Sam wished again...

How many times did she need to put Casey through the tests before she'd accept Casey's blindness as she—and now Brett, the new voice of her hidden shame—needed to accept it?

"Pick up the cups you dropped, Casey," Brett said, the quick excitement fading. "They're all plastic. Seven o'clock, nine o'clock, three and one o'clock. I'll pick up mine."

Casey turned with total accuracy to the dropped cups. Brett watched her, the arrested look returning to his eyes. Sam could see his mind ticking over, working out logistics.

"Put them in the sink, Casey," he said when she'd finished the task.

"You're doing great, princess," Sam encouraged her in a soothing voice. "Watch out for the things Brett dropped. There's no water spilled. You can't slip."

Casey, keeping her head up for balance, shuffled her feet as she moved toward the light that proclaimed the sink's location, near the window. Half her bundle fell into the sink as she opened her arms; the others rolled around the bench top.

Brett spoke, letting the smile of approval come through in his voice. "C'mon, now we've done our chores, we can go swimming again. What game do you want to play?"

Casey's face lit up again. "I wanna play seals!"

Brett took her hand. "Let's go, then." He smiled at Sam as they left the room, with that tenderness that so unnerved her.

Left alone in the kitchen, she washed the picnic gear, shaking. Despite her anger earlier, he was right—she had changed Casey's real name, and he needed to know why. But how could she tell him without implicating his father, who had obviously suffered enough? And Brett thought she was making *him* look like a villain...

It seemed Dr. Glennon had done his parenting research, and was teaching Casey everything she,

Sam, had judged Casey unready for—but in reality she'd been afraid to teach her independence. Michelle had told her that just last week.

Again, all she knew from today's experience was that she wasn't a good enough mother.

And won't that go down well with the rest of the Glennon family when he tells them? The court order will be here before I can say, "I did my best."

She packed up his exquisite picnic basket, put all the leftovers in it and took it outside.

The sight of father-and-daughter rapport left her speechless. Brett had Casey perched against the ladder, remembering her need for security, and he ran back and forth in the water, crashing into her seal with his, making goofy *arrck-arrk* seal noises. Over and over he let Casey dunk him, making gurgling sounds of drowning for her amusement. Casey's delightful silver-and-golden laughter filled the air.

He turned to smile at Sam…and the memories rushed in to haunt her.

So many of their memories revolved around water. He'd taught her to swim on their North Queensland honeymoon—among other things. They'd snorkeled in and around the reef, feeding the half-tamed fish. They'd scuba-dived from a rented boat, searching through shipwrecks and viewing the amazing marine creatures that had made the dead boats their home.

They'd made love in a warm night ocean, just the two of them at their own private beach.

It was too much. White-faced, Sam whirled around and fled into the house.

Brett was in the room beside her ten minutes later. "What is it, Sam? What did I do?"

He'd filled her with pain, and he'd done it almost without a word. With just a smile, he'd made her remember so much…things that hurt to remember. "Where's Casey?" she asked dully.

"In the gazebo. The ladder's pulled up, pool gate locked." He sighed. "Sam, don't lock me out. I can't know what I did wrong if you don't tell me."

She closed her eyes and shuddered. "When I wasn't much older than Casey—maybe eight or nine—one of my foster fathers, the one who played games with me the way you just played with Casey, said…things. I got sent to the orphanage." She gulped. "It's not your fault. You didn't do anything wrong. You're here for her, not me."

She felt the sweet warmth even before his arms wrapped around her; he tenderly pushed her head against his chest. She felt his heart beating against her ear. "My poor Sam. It's over, baby. He's gone…and I will *never* hurt Casey the way he hurt you."

It was dangerous, feeling as if this house had finally become home because he was holding her. "You're here because you're Casey's father."

He dropped a kiss on her hair. "You keep telling yourself that if it comforts you. But I'm going to have you back in my life, Sam. You're my wife, and I *will* make you want it like I do."

"As I said, I am Casey's mother first." She shrugged. "You've tried hard with her today. but I think it's time you left." She added, when he didn't move, "Your basket's by the pool. Please, just take it and go for now."

Brett's jaw clenched. "I know I made a mistake, but it was one Casey didn't understand! I am trying to get this right. Casey deserves to know me—me—mistakes and all."

She rubbed her forehead, feeling very tired. "I need time. You're crowding me after years on my own. That makes every mistake, every memory, bigger than it is."

"The mistake was with *you,* not with Casey," he insisted, his face tight with anger unwarranted to her words. "Stop hiding behind Casey—it's *you*

you're protecting, Sam. This is about you and your feelings of abandonment by your parents. It's not about Casey at all."

Sam blinked and gulped, devastated by his accuracy. "I—I don't want Casey hurt…"

"No, it's you, Sam," he said, gentler now. "And that's the point—*Casey isn't you.* You were abandoned at birth. Casey has two parents trying to make a go of it." When she didn't answer, he kept pushing but without heat. "How many mistakes did you make before you hooked up with the other parents at the Centre? How many times have you unintentionally hurt Casey and learned from the experience?"

Her mouth twitched as she acknowledged the truth. "Plenty."

"So you can forgive yourself, but I have to be perfect or lose out with you both? How long are you going to punish me for your father's sins?"

The hard questions came flying out of nowhere, it seemed, thrusting that emotional mirror back in her face—and she didn't like what she saw.

Denial was no longer the easy out. Being an emotional coward didn't hurt her absent parents, it hurt Brett. And *her* fears of rejection isolated Casey from many people who could love and accept her. She was punishing Brett, Casey and the entire world for the inadequacies that belonged to other people. Brett was doing his level best to connect to his daughter. He wanted his wife, but he wasn't using Casey to get to her, she knew that, if only she was honest with herself.

"I'm sorry," she whispered, leaning back against the sink.

His eyes closed; relief filled his features at her concession. "Is our date still on for tonight?"

Slowly, wanting nothing more than to make an excuse—to plead space, peace, a headache, anything—she made herself nod. "Could you go now? I need space. This is…hard."

"Harder on you than Casey or me…and it's time I knew why, for all our sakes." His gaze was dark, serious. "I need to know about the past six years, Sam."

Feeling brave, she responded in kind. "Just as I need to know about your years in Africa. Don't protect me from it. It only makes me assume the worst of you when things go wrong."

As slowly as she had done, he nodded. "Halfway," he agreed, lifting her hand to his mouth. "We can do this, Sam, if we only want it enough."

But belief came hard to a child reared in the

school of hard knocks; happiness had been too ethereal, too ephemeral. The five months with Brett had a dreamlike quality, her ideal world snatched away too soon…and back to the hard reality of a life alone.

And with Brett's parents she'd received exactly what she'd expected: rejection.

How did she believe life could turn around again? Brett and Casey were the miracles in her life she'd never expected or felt she deserved.

"I'll try," she said eventually.

"Thank you, angel. That's all I ask." And with a soft, brushing of his lips against hers, asking nothing, demanding nothing, he was gone.

CHAPTER NINE

BRETT SWEATED FOR HOURS, working out where to take Sam. But, looking at her face so lit with laughter in the half darkness, he knew he'd made the right choice.

"How did you know?" she asked as they left the theatre for an early supper.

He smiled, aching to touch her. But, knowing she wasn't ready yet, he walked beside her. "You loved the movies while we were dating. I thought maybe you've missed it."

She nodded. "It's the one place I can't take Casey. Other parents have offered to mind Casey so I could go, but—"

Yes…*but.* Like vegging out in front of the TV, the simple right to watch a movie became a difficult, guilt-ridden privilege to the single mother of a blind child. It wasn't the money so much as the *what ifs:* what if I were the one left behind all the time?

By taking her to a silly comedy he'd hoped she couldn't hang on to the guilt. The heroine was insanely in love with the serious psychiatrist, and her earnest attempts to bring him joy were making his life hell…that's what he thought it had been about, but he couldn't keep his concentration off Sam long enough to be sure.

"Didn't you love it when she rewaterproofed his office bathroom?"

"Yeah." He had some dim memory of all the neediest, germphobic psychiatric patients being drowned in toilet water. "She's a real comic talent."

Sam kept laughing all the way down the road, chatting about the movie's high points.

For the first time since he'd seen her again, she was actually relaxing and having fun.

Next port of call was the pièce de résistance. She'd all but forgotten, in her frenetic life, what it was to be a woman enjoying a night out, and no woman deserved more to know it again.

"Oh…" Sam paused as he led her into the plush velvet-lined booth of the old but trendy café. "I've seen this place, going past on the bus, and thought…"

"I saw it today and thought you would love

this." He seated her at the booth. "Why don't you order for us both?"

Having checked out the photos of famous people who'd visited before them on the picture rails, her bright, eager face disappeared behind the menu. "Oh…rum-soaked mud cake…hot chocolate with liqueur in it…"

He grinned. "Still a sucker for dark chocolate?"

She lowered the menu, her smile as bright as the lights lining the street. "Yes…but Casey doesn't like it."

And that settled that. Casey didn't like it, so she went without, with her limited means. He ached to kiss her, to tell her she'd never go without anything again…especially love. If he had his way she'd be bathed in love the rest of her life.

Starting with knowing her—all of her.

While they waited for their order, he said, "Tell me about the past six years for you."

She told her story simply, just stating facts. Coming to Sydney pregnant, alone and without friends. The bewildering array of specialists through the days following Casey's birth. Being kicked out of her flat when Casey just began to walk. Her friend Serena's brother, Colin, coming to the rescue, giving her the house she now lived in at a minimal rent because his blind niece, Kate, was Casey's best friend. Finding friends through the Centre—people who understood her life and made her feel safe. Scrimping and saving every cent she could to give Casey the extras recommended to her by the Centre. Learning to cook and crochet and sing and dance, to raise funds. "I was a clown once," she finished, laughing, "but I only scared the kids who could see me and confused the kids who couldn't. I can't *do* funny."

No, but she could do brave and cheerful and re-sourceful…and never once had she thought to ask his family for money to tide her over. She'd done it all on her own.

Did Sam know how strong she was? He'd faced guns and knives and fanatics with mad eyes, saving people who would probably die within a week. But the 24-7 *responsibility* for the life, health and happiness of a special-needs child was a burden he didn't know if he could have had the strength to carry without family backup, without a trust fund in the bank to pay the bills.

He felt like ordering her a truckload of every dark chocolate variety known to man. He wanted to drown her in flowers, buy her a new wardrobe—

all of the above and at once, to make up for her years of sacrifice for his daughter's sake.

But every day he noticed how many times the word *safe* came up in conversation. That was the legacy he'd given her when he'd left her behind. Being alone and frightened at the most vulnerable time in a woman's life had left her craving emotional safety, especially from him.

He couldn't force the barriers down. He could only show her they existed, and hope.

So he said, "Casey is the confident, intelligent, loving child she is because of you, Sam. You're a damned fine mother and an amazing woman."

Expecting a blush and smile, he was startled by the whiteness of her face and the depth of darkness in her eyes. "I'm glad you think so," was all she said. But something simmered beneath the surface of the words, some mystery he couldn't touch.

Did she still believe he wasn't a good enough father or enough of a man for her?

Love wasn't enough. Sex wasn't enough. He'd studied all the books he could, taken the courses, but none of that touched the reality of Casey and her needs—or Sam's.

His initial insecurity about her hating his lame

leg had passed—he *knew* Sam wanted him. His fears of not connecting with Casey or that she wouldn't fit in with his family had faded. Casey was a Glennon through and through; she'd give as good as she'd get with his parents, and they'd adore her for it.

No. The problem was intrinsic. He didn't *know* Sam. Despite hearing her tale, he hadn't found the core of the woman. He'd admired her strength, her growth, held and kissed her during her rare fragile moments, but until she trusted him enough to let him in and share her deepest fear, he'd remain locked out.

The dessert arrived, a slice of mud cake both of them together wouldn't be able to polish off, and two hot chocolates laced with liqueur.

He used the fork to cut deep into the cake, added cream and moved it to her mouth. "I mean it, Sam. I couldn't be half the parent you've been, and on your own. All my theories about being a good father wouldn't work without you, Sam. You're teaching me to be a parent."

She took the cake into her mouth, cream glistening on her lower lip. He caught his breath as his body took fire. It had been so damned *long* since he'd been with his woman...

She licked the cream away, and his throat got so thick he couldn't breathe. *Sam. Sam!*

"I wouldn't have thought about going to a place like Mbuka to help people I didn't know without you," she said softly. "I'm learning from you, too." She put a forkful of cake into his mouth, her gaze remaining there.

Slowly, in the grip of sensual fever, he touched her still-wet mouth with a finger, trailing it over the touches of cream still there.

Her eyes darkened, grew hazy. Her lips parted. Her soft, fresh scent surrounded him, laced through with chocolate, filling his mind with images he couldn't banish. The needing, the craving was back. Sam, everything was Sam. He had to have her. He had to tell her—

"Trust me, Sam," he whispered, tracing her lips again. "It's going to be so good for us…"

She slowly blinked and returned her gaze to his, level instead of lush, uncertain where it had been sensuous. "I don't know if I can. Not without knowing it all, knowing *you*. I've only heard the barest details of what you've been through. You've told Casey more than me."

Looking in those shadowed eyes, he knew the time had come, but he had to pray to find the strength. "I was doped up when I told her. All I want is to put the whole time behind me."

Her gaze dropped for a moment as her thumbnail went into her mouth—a sure sign that he wouldn't like what she was thinking.

"It doesn't seem like it's working for you," she said quietly. "You're locked in second-stage grief—I learned the five stages in counseling to accept Casey's blindness. You're lost in semi-denial, trying to forget without coming to terms with what happened. Surely the doctor in you knows you'll never be the man you were before or move on without acceptance?"

Thwack. Like a sniper bullet, she'd hit him with the truth so hard he almost physically reeled backward, away from the pain. She'd stripped his veneer of learning and confidence from him, leaving the raw, unhealed, *scared* human sitting before her.

"You know I'm right, Brett." She reached for his hand, her fingers caressing his palm as if to say, *I understand, I've been there.* "Since you've been back, it's like you're almost here but something essential inside you is missing. You talk about what's important for Casey and me—you worry about our suffering, but yours is kept in the dark."

He almost gaped at her. *That's the problem, the reason for her barriers? I've locked her out. She's not refusing to let me in—it's the other way around.*

But all this self-realisation wasn't what he'd come here for, damn it! He'd come here for the beautiful, adoring, *needing* girl who'd made him feel a million feet tall…but this strong, proud, *wonderful* woman with her maturity and wisdom left him stripped and vulnerable. He'd told her enough to realise he needed her. What more did she want from him, blood?

She gave you her blood tonight. When he'd asked about her life, she'd told him.

Now she'd asked. If he didn't talk now, he'd lose her.

He gulped down the hot chocolate without tasting it. "I said I was better with dreams than reality. That was true of my time in Africa," he said, his voice jerky. "I believed I could change the world, but I was stripped of my God complex in days. Half the people who came to me died, and those I saved didn't thank me. They wanted food, family or to get back to the war. Telling people they'd lost arms or legs or that their wife, husband or kids were dead—"

A soft touch on his hand unclenched it. "Go

on," she said softly, but he barely noticed; the darkness had taken him and he couldn't think of anything else.

He swallowed hard. "Or hearing the soldiers or parents abuse me because I couldn't do more. Your illusions die fast. By the time I was shot, I just wanted to get the hell out and get home—" He stopped before he could add, *to you*. "Working for the warlords—" *Damn it, I'm shaking!* "—you're not...human. I worked under duress, guns trained on me all the time, fed only when I was about to collapse. I patched up soldiers and delivered babies, but that had no joy. Boys were destined for training camps, to make their first kill before they turned ten. And the girls—" He shuddered, feeling as if his lifeblood were coming through his pores.

The feel of warm skin against his cheek startled him. Sam had moved around the booth and taken his face in her hands. "I should have been there for you."

He'd waited six years to hear those words, but he took no joy in vindication. "No, you were right. It wasn't the place for Casey." The truth came from a mouth too weary to halt it. "I should never have gone in the first place. I should have been with you, with my family. Then I wouldn't be like this—" he thumped his bad leg "—saddled with baggage I can't—" He shook his head. "I wanted you to heal me, Sam," he said hoarsely.

After a long silence, she moved her hands, caressing his face with tender care. "I wish I could, Brett, but I can't. Only you can. Accept what happened, accept what you can't change, and you'll start to heal," she whispered.

Her lips brushed his on the last word, but he'd turned away, rejecting her words almost before she'd spoken them. "I can't, damn it. *I can't*." His voice cracked on the words. His body language, so tense and withdrawn, was definite rejection.

The night was over, it seemed.

He reached for her, filled with such love and longing he felt ready to explode. "I want you so bad…"

But Sam turned from him. "Sex isn't enough."

Desperate to reach her, to touch her after so many years, he shouted, "I love you, Sam!"

She began fading away. Her voice was a sad whisper. "Love isn't enough. I'm sorry. You have to accept…to heal…"

Brett woke up in the predawn greyness, his heart pounding and sweat all over him. He was grateful that for once she hadn't been blown apart by sniper fire or a land mine, but the ending of the dream had been only little more of a relief.

In a characteristic gesture, he leaped to his feet and limped across the room. His naked body glistened with the sheen of a fear so strong he could feel the sweat rising. He inhaled its acrid tang, tasted its sharp bite.

Tonight he'd found himself loving the new Sam even more than the girl he'd wed. She was a strong, independent woman, full of fire and passionate joy in life. Her haunting fears hadn't abated—he doubted they ever would—but she faced them rather than run. If she was ever going to admit she loved him and wanted a future with him, it would be on her own terms; she wouldn't come down from them or meet him halfway. Sam the girl had accepted whatever he could give. Sam the woman wanted it all or nothing.

It scared the hell out of him. Love wasn't enough. Sex wasn't enough. What did the broken man have to offer her?

Accept what you can't change, and you'll start to heal. How the hell did he do that? He couldn't handle thinking that his life as he'd always wanted it was over—just as he couldn't find a way to accept Casey's blindness was permanent.

Yet seeing a reverse-integration school in action yesterday had taught him so much. The people there didn't look at Casey's lack of sight—they saw her beauty, her sweetness, her intelligence, stubborn independence and competitive spirit. Casey might have the face of her mother, but she had his heart, his spirit, his will to win. She didn't allow life to hurt her.

The pride he felt for her no longer shocked him. Like mother, like daughter. He'd tumbled head over heels for both within days of meeting them. Casey already had him wrapped around her little finger.

But Sam didn't want to believe that. She was still gun-shy.

"So it's time to make her believe," he muttered in determination. He stalked into the shower. Day five of the battle for Sam's capitulation was about to begin.

Accept what you can't change… He'd be damned if he'd accept that it was over for them. *That* he could change—and would if it killed him.

He hadn't yet found the key to unlocking her love, but he had to, to have his family back in Melbourne where they all belonged. Casey needed extended family and the emotional balance of more than one person filling her world. His parents were ready to love and spoil her; it would give Sam time off to do other things in life—for herself as well as him. Casey would enjoy new, broadened horizons. Sam would be happy. And he *would* heal with his family beside him. Soon he'd be able to start his surgical residency and come home every night to his beautiful girls. They'd provide Casey with the baby brother or sister she longed for. Casey was happy but a lonely child. He could see that, if Sam didn't. Casey *needed* his family to complete her world…and some siblings to love and fuss over. He'd provide everything Sam and Casey needed—and they'd do the same for him. Life would be perfect.

Any other ending to this six-year love story was too damn painful to contemplate.

He whistled as he drove to Sam's house, enjoying the leafy way through the hilly, winding streets. Nice place to live in, North Rocks. An abundance of trees and plants in every quarter-acre block, surrounding the comfortable, mellow brick homes of the Australian middle class. Solid, warm, welcoming.

He could be happy here—if he didn't love Melbourne so much.

Sure, it had its drawbacks. Melbourne was a far cooler city than Sydney. You had to dress for its unpredictability; four seasons in a day, they said, and it was true. But he loved the cosmopolitan feel to it, the international flavour Sydney didn't quite manage.

And the family was there, and the contacts he had to gain his residency.

The whirl of the social elite his family reveled in had always been something he'd despised; now it felt mind-numbingly empty. He'd been avoiding his "friends" the past two years, with the exception of a few old school pals, like his mates Denn and Serge.

Denn and his wife Ginny lived in an old terrace by the Yarra River. He and Sam could move into that area—she'd always liked Denn and Ginny, Serge and his girlfriend Grace. They could buy a Victorian terrace somewhere near the water and restore it to original beauty.

He suddenly remembered a dream of Sam's: to buy an old house on the river and redecorate it her way, keeping all the old touches, filling the house with comfortable, livable antiques. He'd let her choose one and let her have her head with the project. She could run wild in the house of her own choosing—not too far from the facilities Casey needed, of course.

Pulling up in the street before the old weather-board house with its four-sided veranda, his tuneless whistling became a rollicking verse. His dream wouldn't happen overnight, but he'd make it happen.

He began the campaign the moment he saw her digging in the garden, clumsy with a massive shirt, big, thick cotton gloves and a floppy hat to protect her from the sun. "Hi, angel," he said softly, leaning into Sam, brushing her startled mouth with his. And the deep, shy blush covering her cheek was all he wanted in reply.

He strolled in the house, knowing the most effective way to make his wife's beguiling gleam of trust focus his way. "Hey, munchkin-head, ready to head for the beach and the most dis-*gust*-ing ice cream of your life?"

"Yeah!" Casey flew around the corner from her room and ran straight into his arms. He twirled her around, laughing, certain now. She couldn't have come to him that way unless she'd seen her path clear to him...

A quick glimpse showed Sam watching. Her smile half sweet pleasure, half aching pain…a smile too brief, too ephemeral, for celebration.

As Sam picked up Casey's scattered toys, Brett lifted Casey up, so her ear was against his mouth. "One day, you and I are gonna have a talk, kiddo, about a little secret I think you're keeping from Mummy."

He felt satisfied by the startled, insecure look on her face; surely that meant he was right. She could see, just a little! "It's okay, Casey-girl. Don't be scared—it's not a crime."

"Don't tell Mummy," the little girl begged in a whisper. "She wouldn't like it."

That puzzled him. Why would she think Sam wouldn't want a cure as badly as he did? "It's our secret, huh? Mummy won't hear it until you tell her."

Casey's face lit up at the words, and Brett knew he'd made a breakthrough. Casey trusted him, and how good it felt. Casey had begun to accept him as her father and she'd just trusted him with the biggest secret of her life.

"I've never swum in the ocean afore." Casey changed the subject as she drew grooves in his dimples with a finger.

He hugged her. "A new experience. Swimming in the ocean isn't the same as being in a pool. You'll love it."

A challenging tilt of her regal little head. "How do you know I will?"

Brett laughed, liking the fact that Casey was no pushover. She had to be won—another Glennon trait. "Something called genetics, kiddo. Your mummy and I love the ocean. We love the waves and the way you float differently."

Casey nodded, her mouth pouting with consideration. "I think I will, then."

"I think I will, then," he mocked her in a high-pitched tone. Casey giggled.

"When you two have finished your morning bonding session, we can leave."

Brett grinned and winked at Sam, who was watching them, still with so many torn emotions in her crystal clear eyes. "Do you feel we've bonded enough for this morning, Miss Glennon?"

Casey giggled again. "I dunno. I want breakfast!"

Casey wriggled down from his hip and ran to eat her breakfast.

Sam's eyes stayed with Casey as she ate her meal with the strict routine blind children need. "Dr. Hauser says she's incredibly intelligent—

she's in step with sighted children her age, which is rare."

Brett turned and looked at Sam, wondering that she didn't *see* what seemed so obvious to him. But he saw only pride and love in her eyes. "You've done a great job with Casey, Sam." He reached out, caressing her face. "I only wish I'd been here to help you."

Sam's eyes, mirrors of her hurting soul, showed the quick flash of uncertainty, the need to believe, the fear this was all a dream. Especially after his reaction to her words on healing last night—it had brought the date to a crashing halt. Then she turned away. "I did okay alone."

The only one who had ever known her heart, he gave her the words he knew she hungered to hear. "Better than okay, Sam. From what I saw at the Blind Society in Melbourne, Casey's well above her age group of kids with limitations. She'd have to be in the top five percent of kids who don't have physical limits."

"Thank you..." The blush filled her averted cheek, staining the delicate paleness of her throat and shoulders. She looked like a young girl being asked on her first date.

But that was his Sam. When it came to understanding that she was loved, she was still as innocent as that young girl.

"Sam," he murmured huskily, turning her face to his. "I only wish I'd been half as successful as you the past six years. All I have is this stupid leg injury. You have a magnificent human life to show for your efforts." He drew her into his arms, feeling the love between them as its own living entity, lighting them both from within. "Casey's a bright, beautiful child who has possibilities beyond anything I'd expected." Holding her with one hand, his other wandered her lovely face. "You're a wonderful mother."

A quiver ran through her as she searched his eyes, looking for truth, for lies—perhaps to see the longing and the love inside him. If she was, she found it. Her eyes darkened from azure to the hue of an evening sky as her lips parted. "Thank you, Brett."

"Samantha," he rasped barely above a whisper, "I'm so hungry for you."

And Sam's pitiful store of resistance died with the words. "Yes…" Her eyes drifted shut as her mouth met his. And from the tenderest of desire, trust was reborn, a crimson blossom unfolding from the palest of buds.

Brett knew—oh, he knew—how to create rapture from the wings of butterflies...

So many memories lay within the realm of Brett's hands. He was evoking them with every provocative movement. Fingertips wafted from cheek to chin, fluttering over her jawline and down, with delicious intent over all her most sensitive zones. Throat, nape, hair, neck to shoulder, arm to hand, fingertip to fingertip, into her palm and wrist, soothing, gentling, caressing.

The desire burst into life, the need for love only he could satisfy. Wanting him came to her with a glance; it could be submerged beneath resentment, loneliness, fear, mistrust. Loving him was harder to ignore. Every memory of love in her life came from him. There was no tender moment, no smiling thought, no time of joy or peace that didn't have its birth in Brett.

Sex she could fight; her craving heart refused to resist Brett's love. Sam basked in the sweet warmth and *safety* Brett enveloped around her. A radiant glow began deep within. Mouth to mouth, hand to hand, heart to heart—she was a dead thing coming to glorious life.

"Sam," he mumbled between kisses so sweet

she knew she'd taste them on her mouth, in her heart, long after they ended.

She burrowed closer, threading her fingers through his hair. "Brett, oh, Brett…"

At her mindless mumble of joy, Brett dragged her against him, moving his tense, aroused body over hers. "Sam, it's been so long…"

"Are we going to the beach now?"

The plaintive question drew them back from their passion, but slowly. Sam rested her head against his chest, holding him close as she gathered her composure.

"We sure are," Brett told her, his voice unsteady. "This is our day out."

A loud sigh. "Then can you stop kissin' so we can go?"

They both laughed. "It's like she can see us," he murmured, testing the waters again.

Sam shook her head. "I know," she murmured. "She always knows what I'm doing."

Keeping it light, Brett sent her a comical grin. "Whoa on that thought, angel, or I'll never be able to have my way with you."

Though she laughed, she quivered again, her gaze luminous on his. "One more kiss."

He gave a low chuckle, lowering his mouth to hers. "Oh, yeah."

Another loud, complaining sigh made them both laugh and part. "Off to the beach for the Glennons," Brett announced, picking up the beach bag Sam had packed ready.

Sam protested as he headed north. "This road leads inland, not to the beaches."

He grinned at her in the rear vision mirror. She was in the backseat again; Casey had insisted on the front seat. "Unless we happen to be going to the Central Coast. Avoca Beach has a lovely little lagoon. It's shaded and usually quiet. It's perfect for teaching Casey to swim."

"Newport or Avalon has an inlet, too, and they're closer."

"I listened to the beach reports. The other night's heavy rain left the water murky. Avoca will be cleaner and less turbulent, too. It's safer for Casey's first time."

"Are we almost there, Brett? Can we get fish 'n chips there? Is there ice cream?"

Brett laughed and ruffled Casey's ponytail. "One question at a time, munchkin-head, or you'll confuse me." He answered all her questions with a patience he'd never known before.

But then, he'd never had a little life looking to him with such sweet trust before…

Touched again by his thoughtfulness with Casey, Sam asked no more questions. He'd thought of Casey first, yet again. It seemed the mantle of fatherhood was falling gently onto his shoulders, and he looked comfortable with the change.

Brett and Casey held a conversation about swimming, picnics and ice cream. Sam watched him grin at Casey again as she asked her twentieth question for the morning, ruffling her hair and calling her "munchkin-head" again.

Casey seemed to like it.

Brett was bonding with his daughter in a way she'd never dared hope. This week had been as beautiful as dreams, as scary as unfulfilled hopes. Brett was making her heart, her body, return to rich, yearning life, with a smile, a look, a single word. He'd always known what she needed to hear—his compliments and names for her corresponding to that need—the unwavering attention to Casey's needs had taken her breath away. It gave her hope that maybe Brett could become the one thing she needed him to be above all others: a good father.

You're a wonderful mother.

He'd said it in a quiet voice full of sincerity, his eyes shining. He thought about Casey as a success, and not in spite of her restrictions.

Sam didn't dare succumb to the gentle whisperings of her aching heart; it could be her body crying out for a lifetime of the shining glory of this morning's kiss, the stormy loving it wouldn't let her forget. So far, Brett's emotional declarations were for her alone. She couldn't allow Casey to be the forgotten third in their love. But with every day, every hour—almost every moment— her resolve weakened. She wanted him—no, damn it, she *loved* him so much…

And she needed him to heal, to accept his new limitations as well as Casey's, or any reconnections they made would be fragile as gossamer and just as easily torn.

Sam sighed with the fulfillment of a hungering soul as the azure of the Tasman Sea came into view. Four years of deliberately starving herself of the ocean. It reminded her too much of the night Brett had proposed, four weeks after they'd met…the honeymoon by the water…the uncontrolled lovemaking she and Brett had indulged in at night…

Avoca Beach was about a hundred kilometres

from Sydney, a shining mass of white sand, curls of crashing azure surf and a much calmer lake-lagoon inlet at its left-hand side. Along the lagoon, the trees that naturally grew there had been allowed to remain, giving shelter and protection to the wildlife still living on its banks. Brett led them to the end of the tree line, spreading a blanket under the shade of the last tree. Slowly, his difficulty level showing the pain he was in today, he bent over to adjust the blanket, and Sam's eyes feasted on the backside and strong legs revealed by the board shorts he wore.

"Your leg should get better eventually, with your fitness levels. You really have kept fit."

His head swiveled around; he grinned at her. "Enjoying the view, angel?"

Caught out in a blatant act of voyeurism, Sam blushed and wrenched her eyes from the sight of him, turning to fuss over Casey's hat.

Warm, strong arms slid around her from behind. "Look all you like," came the husky murmur. "I look at you all the time. I love to know you still want me." He added softly, "Last night…it's a new way of thinking for me. I need time, Sam."

"You have it. Go and spend time with your

daughter." She pointed to where Casey was trying to fill up her bucket with sand.

With a smile, he walked over to where Casey played. As he sat beside her. Casey smiled, welcoming her father into her game. He added dimensions to Casey's lopsided sand castle, finding shells to decorate it, guiding her fingers to them, feeling them, asking her where she wanted them to be placed.

Sam had to turn from the sight. They should always have known each other. If he hadn't forged ahead with going to Africa—

I should have told him I was pregnant. I should have given him a choice.

"Lunch is ready," she called a few minutes later.

The swimming lesson was a success. Casey loved the buoyancy of the salt water, the bouncing of gentle waves lapping her shoulders and feet. She tended to be adventurous, diving under the water, feeling the ocean floor with hands and feet.

Sam held her breath every time Casey submerged. But Brett laughed, encouraged Casey to explore farther afield, reminding her of his presence with his voice and hands.

He looked so proud of her, so…affectionate…

Sam released the breath she was holding.

Maybe she did coddle Casey too much. But she'd never had anyone to love, someone who was hers exclusively—

She was afraid of losing Casey to Brett.

The thought shamed her, but she couldn't change it. Her orphan life had made her heart tenacious and insecure. She loved few people, but those she did, she couldn't let go—ever.

Even though she'd thought Brett dead, she'd never truly let him go.

Her head fell in shame. And she'd been punishing him for wanting her. Had she been sending him mixed messages from the first night?

"What is it, angel?"

The quiet question, full of caring, snapped her from self-recrimination. "Where's Casey?"

He smiled and pointed. "She's found another friend."

Sam started to her feet. "In the water? Are you insane?"

Brett held her back. "She's on the sand, Sam, playing sand castles again—hat on, sunscreen reapplied, protective shirt on," he added, his eyes twinkling.

She jumped to her feet. "I'll go over and introduce myself to the mother."

"No. You won't ruin her moment of independent happiness just to keep Casey to yourself."

The stern words brought a flush to her face.

"You have to stop it. She needs to know what the world holds. You can't keep her protected from all hurt by locking her into the world of the disabled. She won't thank you for it later." He tipped her face up and kissed her mouth. "Casey isn't you, Sam. She's been loved all her life. She'll cope with the rejection so long as she has a loving family to come home to. Let her find her own way and grow into a beautiful, strong young woman, aware of her limitations but not letting them dominate her life— as she surely will if you keep pounding into her that she needs protection from ordinary people."

She felt herself flushing yet again. "Do I do that?"

He nodded, touching her face. "Casey keeps her emotions too much to herself—as you do, Sam. She looks to you for approval, and you give it when she *doesn't* take a chance on life."

She frowned. "But if we're happy—"

He tipped her chin up to face him. "Are you, Sam? Are you really happy hiding from the world, never giving people a chance to hurt you?"

Her gaze fell. She frowned so hard her eyes squinted shut. She didn't need to answer.

"Not everyone will hurt her, Sam. Not everyone will hurt you, either. Most people are pretty decent—and those who turn away are usually embarrassed rather than prejudiced."

"How do you know they aren't prejudiced?"

"How do know they *are?* At least I'm giving them the benefit of the doubt." Tipping her face up to his, he dropped a tiny kiss on her trembling mouth. "Did I do this to you? Did I hurt you so badly that you won't trust any of the human race apart from those who prove themselves to you...or who, by circumstance, understand Casey's limitations?"

Sam sagged. "No," she whispered but wouldn't say any more. She would never speak badly of his family. She knew how he loved them, needed them in his life.

"Don't do it to her, angel." He caressed the palm he held sandwiched between his hands. "Let her live her life to the full. Not everyone's like your foster parents or the orphanage." He gave her a quirky, encouraging smile. "Some are like your friend's brother, Colin, who gives you the house at such cheap rent—or, if they're even luckier, they're like me."

Caught off guard by the little joke, she giggled.

"Look at her, Sam." Brett swept his hand to the glorious sunshine over sand and sea. Casey sat beside a little girl, bearing buckets and spades, busy building. The other girl kept laughing at Casey's lopsided castle but told her where to fix it by guiding Casey's hand to the sand slide.

Casey was laughing.

As if he'd read Sam's mind, he said softly, "Don't deprive her of the chance to know all sorts of people. Some might hurt her—but many won't."

"Five days of fatherhood makes you an expert?" she muttered, feeling stripped. Brett had taken her comfortable mask of protective parenting from her, showing her an ugly truth she might never have faced alone.

Again he surprised her, giving her the reassurance she needed instead of rising to her bait. "You're a wonderful mother, just not perfect. We all need help to learn things we're too close to see ourselves." He lifted her chin again, making her look into his twinkling eyes. "Just as you've done for me this week."

"It's easy for you," she muttered. "You can fix mistakes on a part-time basis—"

He covered her mouth with a finger. "I'm a permanent fixture in your life. And Casey's."

Too scared to believe it, Sam shook her head.

"What will it take for you to believe it?" he asked, low and intense.

Sadly she smiled at him, knowing his answer before she spoke. "For you to heal yourself. To take all the emotional risks you're asking of me and accept who and what you are now."

Without waiting for an answer, she walked over to where the children played to introduce herself to the other child's mother.

By the time Casey was bathed, scrubbed and in bed that night, she was already asleep.

Her nose glowed pink; her cheeks had a touch of sunburn. Her hair, after a day in the sun, even covered by a hat, was almost silver-white. She lay on her bed in violet-pink baby-doll pyjamas, looking worn out, ecstatic even in sleep.

So *beautiful.*

Sam moved to tuck her in, but a touch on her shoulder made her turn to face Brett.

"Go on out and unpack, Sam. I'll tuck her in."

Sam felt too tired to argue, but in a good way. Brett's playing with Casey had given her time to swim in the ocean, floating, indulging her senses. It had mellowed her from her anger...as had the experience in the ice cream store after they'd left the beach.

Brett had read every ice cream label to Casey without embarrassment, letting Casey feel the difference between the baby, plain and waffle cones, paying the vendor for her trouble quietly so Casey's dignity remained intact.

"'Night, munchkin-head. See you tomorrow." After a visible hesitation, he bent and gently kissed the child's forehead.

Sam saw Casey's little hand lift to the spot, a wondering smile lighting her face.

No one had ever kissed little Sam good-night.

The only touch her mother had given her had been to carry her to the church doorstep. Her father probably never knew of her existence—or never cared if he did.

One of her foster fathers had tried to kiss her, and when she'd screamed and hit him, her foster mother had blamed her, called her names and sent her back into the system.

She stumbled out to the bathroom, a hand pressed to her mouth.

A pair of strong arms came around her from

behind as she dry-retched over and over, her stomach aching, her face sickly pale. "Shhh…I'm here, Sam."

She trembled against him but didn't break away. He'd seen her like this too many times not to know how she must be feeling. After his parents had kept her at arms' distance, refusing to accept her as part of Brett's life. When Meghan, his sister, had followed suit, treating her with sweet condescension and careless innuendo. Every time she was shunned at some society function the Glennons had nagged him into.

No matter how many times she tried to be strong, the pain always followed her and hit just as hard. Rejection was the one thing she'd never learned how to shrug off, laugh at or become accustomed to.

When her roiling stomach finally calmed, Brett lifted her from the cold, hard floor tiles, washed her face and helped her rinse out her mouth.

Then he carried her to bed.

Laying her beneath cool sheets, he caressed her face. "Okay?" he asked simply, knowing she wouldn't want to discuss it, even with him. And she nodded.

He sat on the bed beside her. "Want me to stay with you?"

She didn't need him to say he wasn't coming on to her. Brett never made love to her after these times. He'd lie beside her, kiss her, hold her and tell her he loved her.

Her eyes fell; she shook her head. "I'd rather be alone," she said, but she no longer knew if it was truth or lie. She'd been alone so long, her dreams denied…

"Can you get a sitter for Casey again tomorrow night?" His face was serious, intent.

She bit her lip, worrying it.

"I need you, too, Sam," he said quietly, his eyes dark gold with the emotion he'd been holding back—for her sake. He was tired of her avoid-commitment shuffle. He was hurting and he needed her.

Just as she needed him—she knew that now. It was time to take the risks, to reach out and grab at the life she'd been running from for too long.

Slowly she nodded. "Casey's best friend Kate's been wanting her over for a long time. I'll call Serena, her mother."

"Thank you, Sam." After a searching look, he said, "I'll go, then." He got to his feet. Then, like a memory in motion, he bent, kissing her forehead. "I love you, Sam. I always have and I always will."

A warm shiver raced through her. He always knew what to say when she was like this, and he even said it now, when it meant exposing himself to rejection and hurt. "Good night, Brett."

Brett walked to the door. "I'll lock up." As he passed through, he turned. "Casey's a fantastic kid. And...she's part of me...in my heart."

He began to close the door, then pushed it back open, should Casey wake up in the night and want her mother. With a quick, rueful smile, he walked to the front door and left the house.

Then her tears overflowed. But whether she cried for Casey or herself, she no longer knew.

CHAPTER TEN

"BRETT, I'M SO SCARED…"

With infinite tenderness, he hushed her with a kiss. "I know, angel. But this is you and me. This is forever."

The big azure eyes stayed on his, not daring to look down at his nakedness. "I love you."

The words she rarely spoke aloud made his body pulse and pound with adoring love and sheer terror, lest she see how much they meant to him. In one week, his frightened barefoot angel had become the focus and centre of his heart. Now, less than three months later, she was his bride, the holder of his soul, his dreams, his entire life. "I love you, too. I'll always love you, Sam. We belong together now."

He lifted her hand, the one bearing his ring, and kissed it. Then, as she quivered, her eyes full of terrified love, he swept her into his arms and gently made the girl a woman—his woman.

And when the sun rose, the woman he loved beyond life was beside him. In a world of uncertainty Sam was his anchor, his hope, the embodiment of all his dreams.

She moved into his arms with a smile full of love—

Then a sniper rifle touched her temple. a grinning soldier pulled the trigger. "See if you can fix that, doc."

Brett cursed as he awoke, filled with the darkness of memory and only emptiness to comfort him. Why couldn't the damn dreams give him a break for one night?

The memories of the things he'd done, where he'd been and every dead face he'd seen never left him. Every morning he awoke after some nightmare, needing Sam like hell, and she wasn't there. The punch hit him in the guts every day, a mocking reminder of all he'd lost by meeting Sam a few weeks too late. By believing he could have all his dreams and damn the consequences.

So damn arrogant.

The bleeping sound of his mobile phone cut into his self-recrimination. It wasn't even full sunrise yet. With a sigh, he answered, knowing who it would be before he answered it. "Hi, Dad."

"When are you and our grandchild coming home to us?"

"Hello, Dad, how are you?" he greeted his father gently. "Are you okay? How's Mum?"

David Glennon's voice was slightly slurred, the permanent reminder of what losing Casey had done to Brett's family. "Don't be facetious, Brent. I w-want to meet my grandchild. W-when are you bringing her home where she belongs?"

"I'm working on it, Dad. Casey barely knows me yet."

"She's your daughter—"

"Yes, she is." Brett heard the softening of his voice. "You should see her, Dad. She's so beautiful. She looks like Sam but has the Glennon eyes and dimples and all our stubbornness. She's a real bulldog, like her granddad."

The chuckle down the line told him his dad had taken the bait. "She is, eh? So Samantha's allowing you time with her? Has she done a good job raising her?"

"Definitely, Dad. She's a wonderful mother."

There was a small silence. "I w-worried…Samantha had no one to show her the way."

The words were difficult to decipher, which meant Dad was feeling emotional. He was a doting grandfather. Like Meghan's kids, Jenna and Marcus, Casey meant the world to him, even though he'd never met her.

Brett took a few calming breaths. When he'd spoken to his dad, it was all he could do not to book flights to Melbourne for them all, to get Casey where she belonged. But he couldn't, not when his dad's dream coming true could mean the loss of Sam's trust—and Casey's. He wanted his family back in his home by choice. He wanted Sam in his life and bed from love—the love that had never died for a moment for him.

Go slow and easy, was his hour-by-hour mantra. But it was so hard when he was anywhere near the woman he ached for day and night.

"Will Samantha allow us access to Casey?" his dad asked, sounding diffident. "Will she allow you to bring her to Melbourne?"

"I haven't asked yet, Dad. No," he said quickly before his dad could raise the same old argument, "listen to me. She knows I want to bring Casey home, but she's not ready to think about it. She needs to trust me and my motives for asking. I doubt Casey would come with me without Sam. She's only five, Dad, and Sam is her security. There are so many issues with taking blind children away from all they know, Dad. It could traumatise her."

He didn't add that he was doing his dead-level best to woo Sam into being his wife again. His parents knew his feelings only too well. They'd watched in varying degrees of anger, amusement and despair as he'd spent two years and several thousand dollars chasing up every possible lead, paying half the private investigators in Melbourne to find Sam and Casey.

To their credit, David and Margaret Glennon had accepted the inevitable with good grace, doing their best to swallow their anger at Sam's desertion and being willing to welcome her back into the family for Casey's sake.

"Has Samantha thought about returning here? Have you asked her?"

Brett kept the sigh inside. Refraining from pointing out that he'd just answered the question that preyed on his dad's mind all the time and that he didn't know he repeated every three minutes or less, Brett said softly, "We're going out for dinner again tonight, Dad. I hope to get some answers from her while Casey isn't there." He chuckled. "Little imp listens in all the time and then punishes me if I've said anything wrong that she wasn't supposed to hear in the first place."

His dad laughed, as Brett had known he would. "We all know where she got that." The pride in his voice at Casey's being so much like her grandfather rang out loud and clear. "How are you progressing in getting close to Casey?"

"Pretty well." He didn't add what would only upset his father. After two major strokes and four minor ones, he knew not to push his dad's buttons; the emotional stress it brought on could trigger another setback.

"And…with Samantha?" his dad asked delicately—for him.

"I'll know more tonight." *I hope.*

But when he'd hung up from his father, he found he couldn't wait. Without stopping to think—for if he did, he'd end up staying here all day—he dressed and headed for Sam's house.

He gave Sam a comical guilty look as she answered the door with a resigned expression on her face. "I know—but I come bearing gifts."

Sam grimaced, until he held out a loaf of wholemeal bread, a carton of milk, a box of cereal and a bag of fruit. She looked up then, smiling with a touch of shyness. "Thanks, Brett."

"I noticed last night you were running a bit low, and since that's my fault for always being here and eating your food—" He smiled and shrugged, trying to cover the fact that he was aching to kiss that shy smile, to touch her, to make her *crave* as much as he did. "I hope it helps."

"It does." She looked up at him with that bemused half smile she'd worn the night they'd met. "That was thoughtful of you."

The passion he'd forced to bank down until Sam was ready burst into life. The need hummed between their bodies. He saw the aching breathlessness in Sam that signaled her desire. Like the tides changing, it was here, and nothing could drive it back…

Driven along by the force of his craving for her, he bent and kissed her smiling mouth. Fearful of scaring her off, he'd intended to indulge in a moment's aching pleasure. But with a tiny moan, Sam moved into his arms, wrapping hers around his neck. With a groan of pure joy, he dropped the hated cane and deepened the kiss, less in passion than in the love he'd been holding in for too long. The rush of sweetness in a world too hard and bleak filled him with light and love and hope. Finally, after all those years in a war-torn wilderness, he was *home* at last. He was back in Sam's arms, where he belonged.

Well, hell, if he'd known bringing bread, milk and fruit would unlock Sam's heart, he'd have filled the house with it on the first day.

When at last they parted, both of them were breathing hard and fast, both bemused and aroused—and scared.

Sam tried with all her heart to step back, but her arms clung to him, refusing to cooperate. Her body had a will of its own where Brett was concerned. She wanted, *needed* his touch to become the woman she hadn't been in so long, the woman she'd only been with Brett.

His eyes were burning dark with desire and the tenderness that had undone her more than six years ago. And that yearning need in him—the need for *her,* only her—undid her again now. She gave up the short struggle and kissed him again, wrapping herself around him, sinking into the deepness of *belonging* only he could give her.

"Samantha," he muttered against her mouth, sipping at her lips like a bee at nectar. "I've waited so long. I need you so much, Sam…"

But still he didn't push her into passion, content to softly kiss and touch. She caressed his neck and wound a hand into his hair, drowning in the tenderness. "I had to come. I've spent the past six years feeling as if half of me was missing without you. But when I'm here with my girls, it's as if the nightmare is finally over."

Sam stilled. Oh, how she understood his words. And to be needed like that, needed as badly as— as, yes, she needed him—was sweet intoxication. And he'd mentioned Casey without even thinking—it had been simple truth. He was learning to love his daughter.

Her heart whispered its hope to her, and her eager body received and replied to the call. "Brett…" She kissed him again.

"Are you guys gonna kiss all day?" was the interested question from a few feet away. "'Cause I think we just missed the bus to Glenmore Park, Mummy."

Sam gasped and checked her watch. "You're right, sweetie, we did miss the bus."

Brett kissed the wrist held up, smiling at her as her breath caught. Then he turned, smiling. "Hey, munchkin-head. You're right, Mummy and I were kissing. I woke up feeling all lonely today, missing my girls, and headed out here for a kiss better. Now it's your turn. Got a cuddle and kiss for your old dad?"

Casey grinned and flew into his open arms. Her chubby little arms held him tight around his neck. She gave him a smacking kiss, a hearty buss on the cheek—the first she'd ever given him. "Better now?"

Her grave tone got both her parents chuckling. "Much better," Brett said with the same gravity. "So the least I can do is make sure you make it out to Glenmore Park in time for school. You ready? Go pile into the car. Your door is open, four steps in front of the gate."

"Yippee! I like having a dad!" Casey squirmed out of his arms and down to the ground. "I'll get my bag!" She ran for her Barbie backpack.

Sam did a lightning check and was reassured— he'd parked Casey's door exactly four steps in front of the gate. She smiled up at him, melting at his softened eyes because the softness was all for Casey at the moment. "We'd appreciate a ride. Casey wasn't too happy with me when I made you leave the other day. I need to score brownie points with her."

A big, goofy grin covered his face at her admission. "She's really starting to like me."

Sam felt her heart turning all warm and mushy at the look on his face, because winning Casey's love meant so much to him. "You did so well yesterday. I'm sorry I said what I did the day before—"

A finger covered her mouth. His gaze on hers was intent, serious. "We have enough mistakes, hurts and sadness for a lifetime. Let's just go forward from now on."

"All right," she whispered.

"You ready to go?"

It was only when the car door slammed shut that she realised Casey had walked down the path and to the outside world without her watching to be sure she didn't hurt herself. She looked up at him with solemn eyes. "I need Casey's overnight bag. She's going straight to Kate's after preschool, and staying over tonight. She's so excited. It's her first sleepover."

Fire lit his eyes, and she caught her breath as she all but heard his thought. They'd be alone tonight—and could be together all night if they wanted to. "Brett—"

The finger, still on her mouth, moved a touch. "You can't blame a guy for hoping, can you?" His crooked grin warmed her to her toes. "Whatever happens tonight is your call. I'm here for you, no matter what happens. You will learn to believe that."

Again she whispered, "All right," and again he kissed her, long, slow and deep, the passion held at bay. Seducing her with tenderness, until all she could think of was him.

"We're gonna be *real* late if you guys don't stop," an aggrieved Casey called from the car. "You said you was better, Brett! I wanna go to preschool! Get my bag for Kate's, Mummy."

The spell broke with Casey's words. Heaving deep breaths, they parted, foreheads touching. Brett smiled down at her. "Time to go, it seems."

She nodded and moved away to pick up Casey's bag for the sleepover.

Sam felt lost as she dressed for dinner. She was so used to Casey around, following her or needing something, that it was as if her identity had been torn from her, her defining characteristic as a mother. For tonight she would be *Sam,* and she was scrambling to remember what it was she liked or wanted. Who was she when she wasn't being Casey's mother?

She was also experiencing constant bursts of nerves at the thought of being alone with Brett, especially after their kisses this morning. It was as if this was their first date all over again. What if he expected—

This time the stakes were much higher. She couldn't deny the wanting, but whether it should happen was another thing. She had to know what the Glennons wanted, what *Brett* wanted from her and with Casey, if he was going to bring court action to take Casey from her—

If, if, if. Her life at present seemed nothing but *if.* She made an impatient sound, and turned from the mirror.

Her heart started beating like a mad thing when the doorbell chimed.

At first when she opened the door, all she could see was yellow—the bunch of silver-wrapped, gold-ribbon-tied daffodils and yellow roses he held out to her were that big. She felt herself blushing as the lyrics of "Tie A Yellow Ribbon Round The Old Oak Tree" ran through her mind. *If you still want me…*

"You look beautiful, Sam." He couldn't take his gaze from her.

She smiled to hide her attack of nerves.

He smiled back, and her pulse kicked up another notch or five—both at the dimples flashing her way and the elegant understatement of the charcoal suit he wore without the confinement of a tie. "Ready to go? We have a booking for seven. I hope you still like Thai?"

A shy smile filled her face as she nodded. She hadn't had any in so long. Casey didn't like spices, and she could only rarely afford takeout.

"I hear the Star of Spices at Parramatta is an exceptional restaurant. Have you been?"

She shook her head.

"It's BYO. Would you like wine?"

Again she nodded. It would be nice to have wine, the first she'd have in over a year, since a fund-raiser for the Centre.

Brett stepped past her, looking right and left, frowning. "Where's the cat? It came in and took your tongue while I wasn't looking, right?"

She bit her lip, but the laughter bubbled out. "Pathetic joke, Glennon."

"Yeah, I know. Part of my irresistible charm— but it got you talking again." He grinned at her and held out his hand.

Like déjà-vu, their first date had come back around again.

He locked the door for her. "Are you still in favour of white wine over red with Thai?"

"Of course—Thai needs something fruity to balance the spice."

"Good. I bought two bottles each of red and white, just in case." He opened her car door and settled her in. When he started the car, he changed the subject. "I'm glad I drove you to Casey's pre-school again today. Glenmore Park is a fabulous place, isn't it? I find myself constantly amazed by the ingenuity of the people who run these places."

Sam, enlivened by her favourite subject, answered all his questions, totally comfortable in his company. She blinked when they pulled up outside the very trendy pedestrian walk, once a main road but now blocked off with outdoor cafés and stalls, colourful banners and pretty lights and restaurants from around the globe.

She'd walked along the pedestrian walk in Parramatta before, but always before she'd been with Casey. Wistful, unable to describe the colours to her, she'd rushed through it every time, merely telling Casey what place each new scent came from, and what kind of food it was.

Now she was drinking in the atmosphere, the sights, sounds and smells, the friendly smiles and the international ambience, feeling…content. She was here with Brett, and suddenly her colour blindness was gone. The world was filled with vivid hues and visual beauty, and she didn't need to feel apologetic for enjoying its feast.

She was a woman again for one wonderful night and she intended to enjoy every moment.

CHAPTER ELEVEN

BRETT HELD HER HAND, leaning on the cane with the other, but for now, his slow gait didn't bother him. Sam was twisting her gaze this way and that, her eyes wide, taking in all the lights and colours in the bannered walkway, the rainbow-lit stores and in the multitude of people from all parts of the earth. Every few moments she pointed out something to him, looking radiant and so *happy*, he was filled with her light by watching her.

How he'd missed this through the years, being with Sam, *living* more because he saw the world through her eyes.

How long had *she* missed this, too? This was the first time he'd seen her so *alive* since his return to her. He'd seen tenderness and strength and enthusiasm to a degree, but the wide-eyed joy in life had been AWOL.

Is it back because of my presence or because she's free to look at things without guilt?

Whichever reason, he'd make sure the light and life stayed there from now on...and he'd be certain he was the cause of her joy.

Seated in the white-gold-scarlet restaurant, sipping wine as they made their choices, he ordered seafood because he knew she loved it. His angel hadn't disappeared nor even truly changed; she'd just been submerged beneath Casey's needs.

It was time to lift the woman to the surface from her submarinal live-for-Casey-only existence. And it seemed no one else had the ability to do that for her.

He raised his glass at the thought.

"What shall we drink to?" Sam asked, lifting hers.

"To living life to the fullest," he replied, trying to see right down into her soul. Willing her to see that it was all right to be a woman tonight—*his woman*.

Her lashes fluttered down, but her lips curved up as her glass clinked against his.

"Do you think Casey's all right?" she asked once their entrée arrived.

He picked up a paradise prawn to feed to her, but the intimate act she'd accepted just two nights ago with the mud cake made her start like a shy filly. He lifted her hand from the table and wound her fingers through his. "Is the wine chilled enough? Do you need more sweet plum sauce on the prawns?"

She swallowed her food. "It's delicious. Brett, I know Casey would—"

Lifting her hand to his mouth, he kissed her wrist and made a soft, growling sound. "You taste even better than I remembered. Womanhood and motherhood suit you. You're even more beautiful. There's a glow about you that makes me always want to be with you, to touch you."

Her eyes darkened, giving away a passion her words tried to hide. "Casey—"

"Is fine, Sam," he said softly, looking deep into her eyes and seeing the frightened child within the woman. "She's probably playing dollies with Kate and has forgotten our existence."

Sam relaxed and took the second prawn he fed her with his free hand. "Probably." She finished her mouthful. "She and Kate tend to—"

"We can talk about her later." He injected firmness into his tone as he interrupted her. "It's not good for Casey to be the centre of our universe. She has to know we have needs, too."

Sam frowned. "Isn't that a rather selfish view? She's a child—"

"And a very secure one." He lifted her hand to his mouth again. "She knows she's loved, angel. She's happy—probably happier than a lot of kids who have their sight."

"But—"

"There is more happiness in giving than there is in receiving, Sam." He quoted probably the only line from the Bible he remembered from Sunday school. "Don't you get joy from giving to Casey and to the other kids?"

Her eyes lit like a summer sky. "Oh, yes."

"I've always got a buzz from helping others." He tasted her skin again.

Her lips parted as he trailed a kiss along her palm. "You—your face lit up when you talked about Africa. It was…um…inspiring," she added, her voice growing fainter.

He fed her another prawn, repressing a grin at her enjoyment of his touch. "So you agree it's better to give?"

"What?" Her lashes fluttered closed. "Oh… um…yes…"

He tightened his grip on her hand, knowing she'd pull away with his next words. Wondering why he was being such a damn fool in pushing her when all he wanted was to talk about their future as a couple. "Then don't rob our daughter of that joy, love," he said softly.

The spell broke. She gasped. "She's too young!"

Again, knowing he risked emotional suicide here, he pressed her. For Casey's sake. "Remember your first memory of living in the orphanage, besides waiting for your mother and father to come for you, Sam?"

An arrested look filled her face as she lifted her wineglass to her mouth. "We made the decorations for Peter's welcome back party, after his operation," she said, her voice jerky.

"How old were you?"

She almost choked on her sip of wine. "S-six…"

He kissed her hand again and then again, loving the taste of her skin more than any food he'd eat tonight. "Think of the joy she can have from giving to others. She's bright and beautiful, smart and loving. She has a lot to offer the world. Let's allow her to shine." As casually as if he hadn't dropped an emotional bomb in her lap, he started eating. "These prawns are delicious."

"Don't change the subject, having put a guilt trip on me and moving on like it doesn't matter.

You seduced me again tonight—seduced me with wine and food, with picnics and kisses. You've made Casey love you. Am I the next in your campaign?"

The flatness of her expression told Brett that not only had he gone too far, he'd ruined the night for her. She was trembling with suppressed emotion that was in no way sensual. He leaned back in his chair, his gaze on hers, and waited for the rest.

"You're working to plan, aren't you? You came here to take us by storm, then take us home. You want to bring up Casey the Glennon way. I'm a good mother, but I don't have a heritage to give her." She spoke low, trembling with fury. "You've changed her name—with her blessing. Now, with dinner and flowers and wine, you're preparing me for what you really want—your family in Melbourne with you, in the life *you* want, that *you've* planned for us to live!"

Brett swore silently. She'd just dissected his entire campaign with military accuracy; all she'd left out was his goal of making love to her, to make her love him all over again before he took them both back to Melbourne as his accepted family.

As Glennons, where Casey could bathe in the love of extended family, be secure in her heritage and name and the privileges it would bring. Where Sam would be *his* wife, *his* support system as he moved back into the life *he'd* planned for them when he returned from Africa.

But now he saw it as Sam must. Taking Casey away from all she knew and loved—and taking Sam from where she had control of Casey's life and welfare. And she would no doubt be outgunned by his family with every decision she made.

Her accusations struck him with stunning force. Sure, he had ideas for Casey's upbringing, but he'd never once thought Sam wasn't a terrific mother. But from where she stood, that's how it could be interpreted. "I'm in awe of the job you've done in raising Casey. She's a fantastic kid."

Her brow lifted in open cynicism. "Then why is it that we seem to argue about Casey's welfare all the time unless I agree to do everything your way?"

He forced himself to stop a retort. "If I came across that way, I apologise. I'm still trying to learn the basics of parenthood, and you're so good at it, so natural, it makes me feel inadequate."

Sam's mouth opened and closed. "I see." Her frown not quite so deep now, but her eyes far away. "And there's no other reason?"

"Does it have to be complicated? Sure, there are

things I think could change, but you think that about my ideas and methods with her. Meeting halfway and giving our child what the other parent doesn't have—isn't that what shared parenthood is about?"

"You would be willing to compromise." It wasn't a question.

He decided to take a quick plunge. "On anything you want, Sam—anything. If it gets me what I want, I will do whatever it takes."

She kept her gaze clear and strong on him and didn't pretend to misunderstand his words. "By that you mean me?"

"You—and Casey," he agreed, stroking her palm with his finger. "I want my family. I want you both in my life, permanently, daily, hourly, sharing my home, my life—and you, sharing my bed. Having more kids. I want the whole nine yards, Sam, and I want it with you."

She let her hand lie in his, her gaze steady. In the red-glass flickering candle between them, she looked lovely, fragile as that glass yet strong as tempered steel. "And if I say I won't return to Melbourne? That Casey and I are happy here?"

She'd thrown the gauntlet down with a vengeance. "My life, my family is in Melbourne," he said, feeling his way around the sensitive issue as Casey would do in unfamiliar territory.

"Then go home to them if they're your first priority, Brett," she said quietly.

His gaze searched hers. "Is that what you want, Sam? Do you think that's what Casey will want? And will she thank you for it when I'm gone?"

Sam flinched.

Instead of pleasant conversation, this night had become one of risks—and now he must take another. "I know you want safety, Sam, but will it be worth the price you pay when Casey asks why I went and if I have family she can meet? Because I won't go and never come back." He drew in a breath. "I'm a permanent fixture in Casey's life, no matter what happens with us."

The waitress served their main dishes and a bucket of jasmine rice, big enough for them both.

He waited until they'd eaten before he spoke about anything but the food and wine, giving her time to think. But Sam started before he could. Her mouth twitched as she put down her fork. "You want it all, don't you? You still believe that your dreams and wishes are best for everyone."

His knee ached; he let his left hand drift beneath the table to massage against the swelling. Far from a night of romance and coming together, Sam seemed determined to sabotage it—

Was she trying to make him lose his temper and leave?

He kept his tone even and reasonable. "My family is there, Sam. We both grew up there."

Her brows lifted again. "So one of us has happy memories of Melbourne. I personally never want to go back."

"We were married there," he reminded her quietly. "We had friends, a life."

"Your friends," she replied, just as quiet. "*Your* work, *your* life; your plans. Everything was yours. I just went along for the ride." She shuddered. "I learned you were dead there. They... locked me out. I was never good enough for you, even for Casey. I had to get out..."

He caressed her hand and his knee at once; it seemed they both needed comfort. And he needed to think. Her words had been raw, from a heart unhealed by the time they'd been apart.

Something was wrong? Something had happened in Melbourne she wasn't talking about.

They locked me out...not good enough, even for Casey...

The subtle pressure his family had put on him

during the past year to divorce Sam and find a "more suitable" wife took on new meaning. And suddenly with crystal clarity his mind unlocked the doors of the past he'd kept guarded with Bluebeard-like jealousy. All the things he hadn't wanted to see came back to haunt him.

Meghan's refusal to become friends with Sam. *We're just too different, I suppose.* His parents telling her at some function they'd bludgeoned them into attending, "No need to tell anyone where you came from or grew up, dear. Just say something polite if they ask who you are. You know how to do that, don't you?"

Introductions had been a small nightmare. *This is our son, Brett. He's a doctor and signed up to serve in Africa. He will eventually become a top surgeon. Oh, yes, and that's his...*friend, *Samantha.* And when the word *friend* had become *wife,* they'd always used a three-second hesitation before saying it when introducing her to anyone.

How had he forgotten the times Sam had smiled to hide the tears?

There was only one answer to that: he'd loved his family, and had chosen to bury the pain...and then he'd gone to Africa, leaving Sam to their mercy, trusting in their innate kindness and love for him to smooth over any rough spots.

Yet they'd given all those subtle digs when he'd been there to protect Sam, to correct them when they'd hurt her. *I suppose we just don't understand her life.* If they'd been so unkind when he'd been there, how had they treated her when he was gone, presumed dead and no longer a bulwark against their careless hostility?

You're not taking Casey from me!

The *fool* he'd been not to see it. So many reasons to have left the Glennon home, but nothing else could have made Sam change names and states. In their grief, his parents would have done anything to have his child safe under their roof.

Finally he understood what he was up against. Why would Sam ever want to go back to face more of the same—and to fear the same rejection that could be in Casey's future? Or to have her decisions for Casey overruled by the sheer weight of the mighty Glennons, including him? She probably feared being edged out of Casey's life altogether, a satellite mother whom even Casey would eventually feel was not good enough for her.

God help him, where did he go from here now that his last, most cherished dream—of becoming a surgeon in Melbourne, with his wife and daughter to come home to, part of the Glennon clan—had just crashed and burned at his feet? And more importantly how could he ever make it up to Sam? All she'd been through, all the years of neglect and blame!

"Brett? Are you all right?"

He snapped out of his dark thoughts and smiled. "I'm fine."

"I didn't mean to—"

"Yes, you did," he said quietly. "But it needed to be said."

Sam bit her lip. "I—"

"No, don't, Sam," he said, his gaze calm on hers. "Let it go."

She closed her eyes and nodded. "Is your leg paining you?"

Relieved to be able to answer that truthfully, he nodded. "No dancing for me yet, it seems."

She looked worried. "Why hasn't it healed properly? Could you handle the physical exertion of hospital work, especially given the understaffing problems in Australian hospitals?"

He gritted his teeth, willing her to stop killing his hopes for the future. "Thanks for caring, but I hear enough of that cheering news from my therapist. If I can get a little faith, a little hope that it can happen for me one day, it might be helpful."

Her face hardened. "Sorry to upset you. It's none of my business, is it?"

Brett swore aloud. He'd cut her dead just when she'd allowed herself to care about him, and all for the sake of his stupid pride, keeping his foolish dreams alive. She was right—he was hanging on to dreams even he had begun to doubt lately. He'd held on so tenaciously because he didn't know what the hell to do with himself if he couldn't be a surgeon.

Whose fault is that? I didn't have to go to the worst part of Africa to help. I could have listened to good sense and picked somewhere safer.

On hearing a small, stifled noise, he refocused to Sam. She was blowing her nose—her way of avoiding tears.

So much for convincing her they would be happy together! He couldn't even manage to give her one happy night. If there was any other way he could hurt or alienate her, he was sure he'd find it next. "It is your business. You're my wife, and—" he hesitated; this was so damn *hard* "— and you're right. I have to learn to accept that I'm far from perfect, Sam. Not perfect as a doctor, not a perfect father—and a far from perfect husband," he muttered, low. "I left you to their mercy. I should have known what they'd do to you."

"It's all right." With her dessert spoon, she traced patterns on the red paper covering the white tablecloth.

"No." With a supreme effort, he held back from snarling. "It's not. Not for them to hurt you that way—and not for me to have left, assuming everything was fine. Assuming *I* deserved the comfort from *you* while your life fell apart. I should never have gone without you."

"It's over, Brett." Her eyes turned dark. "We need to move on from here. To accept our past before we can know if there's a future for us as a family."

"Oh, there is, Sam." He picked up her hand and kissed it. "Acceptance is good. Such as accepting that we have a future together, that I'll always be here for you from now on or accepting how much I love you."

He saw her swallow and worry the inside of her lip. "Brett—"

"Tonight I'll show you how much we have in common. Including the fact that we both lose our appetites when we're upset," he went on as though she hadn't spoken, smiling at her in the way he knew always melted her resolve. "I'll ask them for a doggie bag. We can take it home—if that's what you want, Sam. If it *is* home for us both." He didn't make it a question, hoping like crazy that she'd take up his suggestion.

"And?" she whispered, eyes fixed on his face. The pain was still there, but her lips had parted when she'd seen him smile—and anticipation was there, too.

She was listening…and maybe, just maybe, she was open to his suggestion.

"And we could start over and pretend we never came here. Drink the rest of the wine, eat the food, And I'll hope like crazy I haven't blown it with you tonight, while Casey's gone."

"In other words, the night isn't over yet?" she asked softly, her gaze soft and warm now, the anticipation growing every moment.

He looked into her eyes and his whole body took fire. By taking that emotional risk, by accepting his limitations, he was winning—but more than that, he was winning her over. "Not by a long shot, angel."

If he had his way, the night would blend into tomorrow, the next day, week, the next year or decade—in her home, in her bed.

He just prayed he didn't blow it again.

CHAPTER TWELVE

WHAT AM I DOING?

Sitting beside Brett as he nudged above the speed limit to get home sooner, Sam wondered if she knew her own mind. She could tell by his anxiety—by the way he looked at her as if he wanted to devour her whole—that there hadn't been anyone else in his life or bed. But that, strangely enough for her, she'd never doubted.

How did his family feel about his renewed courtship of her?

"How many eligible girls did your parents and Meghan introduce you to in the past two years?" she asked him softly.

He lifted the hand he still held to his lips. "None that interested me, angel."

"I know that." She smiled at him. "That much I've known all along, Brett. You always keep your promises."

"Thank you." He sounded moved by her faith.

She pressed her lips together for a moment before she spoke. "You know this isn't set in stone, don't you? That whatever happens tonight doesn't mean that we'll be together forever?"

Expecting a flare of anger, she was surprised when he nodded. "But it's a good step, and one you wouldn't make if you weren't thinking seriously about us, Sam."

He didn't put his thoughts in question form anymore. The old commanding Brett was back, leavened with the quirky humour she loved so much. And she couldn't blame him for being sure of her. He was right. She could never sleep with a man she didn't love.

And she would *never* make love with a man who didn't love Casey—and Sam could no longer deny Brett's love for his daughter. Not when he'd put his chances of being in her bed tonight down to zilch by pushing for what was best for Casey. He'd fought for Casey's needs, put them above his own—and in doing so, had blasted all her defences to rubble.

For the first time, her terrified soul listened to what her heart had been telling her from the start. He truly loved Casey. He would never hurt her intentionally, never reject or ridicule her.

Strange that his alienating her made Sam so sure that taking Brett back into her life and bed was the right thing for them all—but he'd done it for Casey's sake, risking it all to make Casey's life better, and that made the difference.

"We're here."

Startled, she looked at the house, softly lit and welcoming, as if it had known the outcome of tonight more than she had done. And then she looked around at Brett. It had been so long…

His brow quirked. "Changed your mind? We can just have coffee and I'll go…crazy, but I'll go."

His eyes were burning hot. He looked at her like a starving man faced with a banquet. Using humour to hide the fact that making the offer was killing him—and if he was half as hungry for her as she was for him, she could relate.

And in making the offer, he touched her soul. He really cared about her feelings in a way he hadn't when they'd married. Then, her life had been Brett's, his decisions good enough. Now he respected her opinion and abided by her rules…and something told her it wasn't an act that would end once he'd returned to her life and her bed.

She leaned over and brushed her mouth on his. "If I had, you just changed it back for me."

"Thank God for that," he murmured against her lips, kissing her between each word.

"Let's go inside." She handed him his cane and grabbed the bag containing the leftover food and wine.

"I'll take that."

She gave him a look filled with yearning and mischief combined. "I'd prefer your free hand to be touching me, if you don't mind."

His eyes blazed. "After six years not touching you, try keeping me away."

Laughing, touching and kissing, they made it to the door. Sam dropped the key twice, fumbling with the growing excitement and *beauty* of being a woman, of being his woman. He growled with impatience, having to use one hand to hold on to the cane. Finally they made it inside the door. She slammed it shut and moved to the buttons on his shirt as he dragged her close, kissing her ear—

Then the sound she hadn't truly heard came through. Someone was leaving a message on the answering machine.

"…I'm sorry, Sam, but Casey woke up screaming for you. I'd bring her home, but now Kate's upset, too, and I can't handle them both crying all the way over. Can your husband come and get her? Casey's screaming for him, as well."

Sam was at the phone before Serena had time to hang up. She didn't need to ask Brett if he'd drive her; he was right beside her, the remains of passion in his eyes fading beside concern for Casey. "We'll be there in ten minutes, Serena. Sorry, we just got in," she said, noticing the flicking number two on her message machine. "Tell Casey we're on our way."

Despite his bad knee, they were in the car within moments, heading west to Serena's house.

Brett was tense on the drive, his gaze fixed ahead.

"I'm sorry about this," she said tentatively. And heaven knows, she *was* sorry for them both. She'd wanted him so much, needed the closeness of their loving.

"No need to be." He shook his head. "The latest research indicates that severely sight-limited children, while as young as Casey, only have nightmares under extreme stress. Dreams are visual things. She must be really upset about something to have a nightmare." He glanced at her, frowning deeply. "Do you think it's us? Doesn't she want this to happen for us, Sam?"

Her hands fluttered up in a gesture of helplessness. "She's never said anything to indicate she doesn't want you with us, Brett."

"Has she had nightmares before?"

"Night terrors," she said slowly. "She hasn't had them for a while, but night terrors are natural in the blind. Changes trigger them."

"Me bounding into her life?" he asked grimly.

"No, I don't think so. She usually reacts faster than that. I think it's staying over at an unfamiliar house. Serena would have walked her through it, but even a stubbed toe is enough to give her an attack." She touched his hand. "Stop blaming yourself, Brett."

"How can I not?" He shook his head and sighed harshly. "I knew all this statistically, but I still charged into change her world, forcing myself on you both—"

"You've made her life better," Sam said, slow and definite. "I know that now, Brett. I won't block you taking her to meet your family, if that's what you want."

She held her breath, waiting for the usual take-charge Brett to insist she come with them and make a family. But, caught in self-recrimination and worry for Casey, he merely said, "If she'd trust me enough to come. If I'm the cause of this terror—"

He pulled up in front of Serena's house and leaped out almost as soon as he'd stopped the car.

Sam watched him go to the door at as close to a run as he could with the cane. She followed a step behind. The moment Serena opened the door, they could hear Casey's half-hysterical cries.

"Mummy! *Mummy*! B-Brett! *Brett!*"

Dropping the cane, he strode toward the quavery cry from the living room. Casey sat on the sofa, wrapped in a blanket despite the warm night, her face white. "Hey, munchkin-head," he greeted her in a gentle, soothing voice. "Did you want to come to dinner with Mummy and me so badly you had dreams about being left behind?"

He'd already sat beside her and gathered her into his arms, caressing her tangled mop of curls. But Casey climbed right into his lap, burying her face in his chest and sobbing incoherent words. Brett's eyes closed; his face softened with love yet held the residual tension of fear. He rocked her back and forth, keeping his words tender and reassuring.

Holding his forgotten cane, Sam watched them from two feet away, giving them time and space, giving Brett the right to comfort their child. Casey would be fine now.

On tiptoed feet, the turning point in her life and relationship came to Sam—because Brett was putting Casey first. He hadn't pushed in front of Sam to impress her; he'd been too worried for that. As he comforted Casey, he never glanced once in Sam's direction. He was acting on pure instinct and getting it right. Nestled securely in the arms of someone she loved and belonged with, hearing the soft nonsense words of loving reassurance, Casey was calming down, her sobs downgrading to tiny hiccups.

He was a true father.

She was free, free to love him once again. She'd even face the Glennons en masse, with Brett beside her, for finally his silence in the past made sense. *Let her learn to cope with failure and rejection, Sam. Don't limit her from being all she can be.*

She could always have spoken back to the Glennons when they'd patronised her. Brett had always stood beside her, waiting for her to speak, to find her confidence with the family. He'd believed in her. But she hadn't believed in herself. She'd wanted a hero and she'd had one in this man who'd known what she'd needed and waited for her to discover her own strength.

Slowly she came to sit beside him on the sofa

but didn't touch Casey or signal her presence. She was here; Casey knew that. When her daughter needed her, she'd come.

"Let's take her home," he whispered when it seemed Casey had fallen asleep. But when he tried to hand her to Sam, Casey whimpered, clinging to Brett.

He sent her a helpless look. How could he carry her?

"On your good side, on the hip," she whispered. "She'll hang on. She always does. I'll be on your other side."

He nodded. "Can you drive? I'll hold her."

With a few murmured thanks to Serena and a promise to have Kate over to play soon, they headed for the car. Casey was wrapped around Brett's right hip and shoulder. Sam held his cane and walked beneath his left arm, holding him up in case his knee gave way.

And Sam finally understood the one basic truth only life could teach the orphan child: this was how a family should be, working together and supporting each other.

In the car, Casey wouldn't let go, becoming hysterical again when he tried to move for a moment. Brett struggled as he strapped her into a seat belt, but he left his off so Casey could hang on to him. He nodded to Sam. "Let's go."

She drove home carefully, and not just because it had been years since she'd driven anywhere. Casey was safe, but Brett wasn't—and without him, her life would be as empty as it was before. She loved him so much.

At home, she didn't take over, merely lifted the bed covers so Brett could put Casey to bed. "You're home, munchkin-head." Brett's voice was filled with love. "You're safe. We're here."

But Casey tossed and turned, holding on to him so tight Sam could see the sweat breaking out on his face with the pain of the awkward position. "B-Brett…"

"What is it, Casey?" he asked through gritted teeth but with a voice still filled with tenderness.

"K-Kate said her daddy stopped visiting her when he got married and had other kids…"

As if a candle had been lit within his soul, his face glowed. *Casey loved him*. She wanted him in her life. When he spoke, his words were firm, in contrast to the look of utter adoration on his face. "Listen to me, Casey Amelia Glennon. *You are my firstborn child, and I love you. I will never leave you.*"

And the three words he hadn't spoken to Casey until that moment penetrated the heart of the insecure child. Slowly she stopped thrashing in the bed. Her sightless eyes gazed up at the man who'd changed her world forever within a week. Asking the question without words.

"Yes, I love you, you big, dopey munchkin-head," he repeated himself, voice strong and stern. "Got that?"

Casey nodded, a big, radiant smile covering her sweet face.

"Good, because that's guaranteed for life. And any other kids your mummy and I might have will need their big sister to show them things and to take care of them."

"You won't have kids with another lady? If you have kids who can see, you'd like them better, right?" she asked timidly.

Sam gulped down a burning ball of emotion. Brett had been right—she'd been infecting Casey with her own fears.

"Never," Brett said, taking Casey's hand and placing it over his heart. "Scout's honour. I love your mummy, Casey, as much as I love you. Any brothers and sisters you have will be right here, in this family. I love you, Casey. Just as you are."

Casey's whole body relaxed from its trembling. With a sigh, she slid down onto her pillow. "Stay with me," she whispered.

With a helpless look, Brett reached into his pocket and handed Sam the bottle of painkillers. "I wouldn't want to be anywhere else." Sweat was trickling down his temple with the pain, but he turned back to Casey and snuggled in.

Sam's heart almost burst with love for him. She bolted for the kitchen and a glass of water.

When she came back, Brett was talking to Casey as she slid into sleep.

"I have bad dreams, too, Casey."

"I know. You did the night you slept in my bed," Casey mumbled against his chest.

"Oh." Brett's face clenched as the pain gripped him again. "I'm sorry, Casey. Some things I saw made me scared and sad, and I just keep seeing them over and over at night. But when I'm with you and your mummy, they kind of fade away. So I wouldn't leave you for the world. I know how it feels to be so scared and wake up alone."

"Okay." Casey sighed and snuggled in a bit closer. "I'll make you better."

His heart gripped tight with love. "You already do, munchkin-head."

"Brett, do you think I should tell Mummy about Ryan?"

He blinked. "Ryan?" he asked, trying to understand this sudden curveball.

"Yeah. My secret. My boyfriend, Ryan."

Brett felt his brows lift right into his hair. Oh, God help him for being so stupid! He'd thought Casey had some tiny portion of sight—he'd hoped it, believed it, trying to cling to his dream that she could be cured and become as perfect as she promised to be.

Her secret was a *boyfriend?*

And though his heart ached that he'd been wrong—that her life would always have the limitation of blindness, and he, the doctor who'd always dreamed of being a miracle worker, could do nothing to change that, as he couldn't change his own limitations—he wanted to smile. Casey had a boyfriend.

Right, daddies coped with this kind of mini crisis daily, didn't they? He tried to unscramble his brain. "Is he one of the kids at the Centre?"

"At Glenmore Park. You met him, don't you remember? He says I'm beautiful."

"He's one of the sighted kids?"

"Duh," Casey mumbled. "He couldn't say I was beautiful if he couldn't see me, could he?"

"I guess not." Another wave of pain gripped him. Where was Sam with those painkillers? "Why do you think Mummy wouldn't like it, Case?"

Casey yawned again. "Mummy doesn't like the other kids. The ones who aren't like me. And she doesn't like it when I don't stay with her."

A tiny sound came from the other side of the door. Brett turned his head. Sam stood just outside the doorway, biting her lip and screwing her face up in rueful acknowledgement of the words Casey had meant for her to hear…because she always knew when her mother was nearby.

Casey needed him here to diffuse the hurt it would cause Sam. She'd *needed* him.

Quietly Sam came in and handed him his pills and water, which he gulped down while she spoke. "I'm sorry, Casey. I haven't been very nice to Ryan, have I?"

Casey shook her head. "And he's *real* nice, Mummy."

"You really like him, huh?"

"I *love* him, Mummy. He's my boyfriend!"

The indignant words made both her parents smile, but Sam kept her tone grave. "Of course you do. I'm sorry, Casey. How about we have Ryan over here to play soon?"

"Can he sleep over?" Casey asked eagerly.

"No way." Brett made his voice firm. "No boyfriends stay over. Only girls can sleep over. That's a daddy rule. Ryan can come to play and stay to dinner, but he goes home at night."

"Okay," Casey mumbled, sounding a bit resentful but accepting. "I want to sleep now."

Sam feathered a kiss on Casey's forehead. "Good night, sweetheart."

Then her lips brushed Brett's with sensuality that seemed deliberate to him, a promise he couldn't possibly misinterpret. She smiled and left the room, her hips swaying.

Brett got the message, all right—and he hoped like crazy those painkillers kicked in without putting him to sleep.

After an hour, when the discomfort of lying still in a single bed with Casey taking up most of it was likely to kill him, he slowly edged off the bed. She rolled over and mumbled something but didn't wake, and he took that as a good sign.

Was Sam still awake? If her door was shut, he'd take that as a sign, too, and take off—if he could.

Though the painkillers had done their job, the hour or more of discomfort holding Casey had left the knee weak. Where had Sam put the cane? If he couldn't find it, he'd just sleep on the sofa, short as it was. He wouldn't take anything for granted.

Finally he'd learned the lesson, including taking his dreams for granted. His knee might never heal as much as he wanted it to. He had to learn to accept what was less than perfect…and he could do that, because if he had Sam and Casey in his life, he had more than enough.

The dreams had played their part. He wondered now if it was his subconscious telling him what was most important. The wandering refugees in Mbuka knew more than he had. It had taken losing everything most important to him before he recognised the truth.

Without family, without love, no dream was worth squat. He could live without being a surgeon. He could live outside of Melbourne. What he couldn't live without was the woman he loved more than life and the child who'd grabbed his heart with both hands.

Where was that cane?

"Hi. Going somewhere?"

He swung around toward the soft, husky voice.

Sam stood in her bedroom doorway wearing a smile, a summer-short nightie and nothing else. She crooked a finger. "Come here."

Brett made it to her in Paralympic-record timing. "Sam," he breathed as he dragged her close to him, half-afraid this dream would shatter in his face.

Her eyes remained on his, the tenderness taking his breath away. "I'm sure, Brett. I've never been more sure of anything in my life."

"I love you," he said, quiet, intense.

"I know." Her mouth brushed his. "You know, too. You always knew."

She broke the deep, heated kiss to hang a small sign on the door, covered with words in Braille. *Do Not Disturb* in Braille. "Her night terrors are over, for tonight at least. It's our time now," she whispered. Then she took his hand and led him in, closing the door behind them.

CHAPTER THIRTEEN

WHEN THE MOBILE PHONE bleeped just before sunrise, Brett was ready.

He'd spent the past hour or more just thinking as he'd held Sam close. They'd made love half the night, kissing and talking when they were not, connecting in the love she hadn't spoken before this night. He suspected she was awake, too, and waiting for the inevitable, but she refused to influence his decision. She hadn't told him exactly what they'd done to her, but he knew.

"Hi, Dad," he greeted his father. Unlike many stroke victims, David Glennon was always up before the sun. "How are you today?"

"When are you coming home with my granddaughter?"

"I'll ask Sam and Casey about it and give them the choice. When they're ready to come, I'll let you know."

"I want to m-meet my g-granddaughter *now,* damn it!"

Brett closed his eyes, imagining his father's face reddening, his veins standing out.

His dad was bringing this on himself because he couldn't stand to be thwarted.

Taking a massive risk, he said, "I know what you did to Sam, Dad. I know how terrified and insecure you made her feel." He heard Sam's little gasp but kept speaking. "I won't ask her to come back to Melbourne to face more of the same unkindness from you all."

A strained silence followed before David Glennon spoke. "I don't know what the h-hell you're t-talking a-bout. What did I do?"

Brett was startled into silence. Oh, hell, after six strokes, his dad wouldn't remember what he'd done to terrify Sam. "Put Mum on the line, please, Dad."

When Margaret Glennon's half-sleepy mumble came on the line, Brett greeted her briefly before he repeated what he'd just said to his father.

"I thought she'd tell you," his mother said with a touch of acidity when he'd finished.

"Sam didn't tell me anything. I worked it out from all the things she didn't say." He looked down at Sam, still nestled in his arms, with pride and love. "She won't say a word against my family, Mum. She loves me too much to hurt me."

Tears trickled out from beneath Sam's closed lids.

"I see," his mother said eventually. "So you want to know what happened."

"And why you didn't tell me before," he agreed.

"I'm just taking the phone outside. Your father doesn't remember anything, and it would only distress him to know." After a few moments, she went on. "Your father was convinced that Samantha didn't know how to be a good mother. It kept him awake nights when she bought secondhand furniture for the baby, refusing to take our money to buy new. He was worried she'd do other things to risk the baby's health. He insisted she live with us. But within two weeks he was fretting at her swimming regime and her diet. He threatened her with a court order gaining custody of the baby—he said he'd prove her an unfit mother. Samantha disappeared that night, having emptied your joint bank account before she moved in. She only stayed with us to prove to you that she'd tried." Her voice was a touch acidic as she finished.

"Well, that was more than you, Dad or Meghan did," he said gently for the sake of the woman working around the clock to keep her husband safe and happy. "Can you say you ever tried to know her or accept her into the family except as the carrier of your grandchild?"

The silence was stricken.

"I won't be bringing Sam and Casey back to Melbourne unless they want to come. They have a happy life here in Sydney and have no reason to return to Melbourne...unless you can give them a reason. Unless you can give Sam a reason to believe she'll feel welcome and secure in the family," he said quietly, with finality.

"You're going to *live* in Sydney?" his mother asked, sounding terrified.

Smiling at Sam again, he said, "If Sam and Casey want to be here, then I want to be here, too. My knee won't stand up to the pressure of being a surgeon for a few years yet. I can become a general practitioner. I might as well make use of my skills to help people and provide for my family, as Sam has done for Casey the past five years."

Sam buried her face in his chest, taking deep, heaving breaths. He kissed her hair.

His mother sounded stiff. "I realise you're angry with us, but we were just protecting our family, Brett."

"Then you should understand that I'm protecting *my* family. You can't stand Dad being upset. I won't tolerate Sam's being hurt or excluded again. I love her, Mum, just as you love Dad. She's my wife and she will come first with me from now on."

"Your father—"

"Dad will learn to cope with failure, just as the rest of us have to. No tantrum or fear of another stroke will change my mind," he said, gently cutting short the guilt trip. "Tell him, Mum. He will see Casey when you are all prepared to make my wife truly welcome."

Sam looked up at him, her eyes shimmering, luminous. Never had she looked more beautiful than this moment. "I love you," she mouthed.

I love you, too, he mouthed back.

"Brett, I don't think he can change," his mother said, sounding desperate. "He's forgotten it all and is prepared to tolerate—"

"*No*." The single word cut his mother short. "I will not ask Sam to *tolerate* your snobbery again. Either you welcome us all or you miss out on knowing Casey." He softened his voice. "And Casey's worth knowing, Mum. She's so beautiful. She's adorable, like her mother, and damn-fool stubborn, just like her dad and grandpa," he added for effect. "Sam's done an amazing job with her. You hardly remember she's blind, she's so smart. And she doesn't feel sorry for herself. I'm damn proud to be her father—and you'll be proud to be her grandmother, Mum. I guarantee it. She's the best kid in the world."

In the silence, Sam wiped her eyes. "I'll get us some coffee," she whispered.

"Thanks, sweetheart," he replied loud enough for his mother to hear. With a brief kiss filled with tender gratitude, she left his arms, got to her feet, dressed and pulled open the door.

And Casey stood behind it with a smile so radiant it stole his breath. She'd been listening in again, the little monkey—but this time she was lit up like the Parramatta walking mall.

"Hey, munchkin-head," he greeted her, giving his mother time to think and to realise where his priorities now lay.

"Thank you, Daddy," she said softly, her radiance a thing of beauty far beyond her pretty features. "Thank you for being such a nice daddy."

Sam bit her lip. Tears flowed down her beautiful face, and he knew the final barrier was broken. "Come here, Case," he said, gruff with unshed tears. "Give your dad a hug."

Casey flew into his arms, hugging him tight, but it didn't last long. "Is that my nana you're talking to on your phone?" she asked, her interest caught. "I heard you say 'Mum.'"

"Yeah." He looked up at Sam, who smiled and nodded. "Want to talk to your nana?"

He handed the phone to Casey. He knew his parents; after talking to Casey for a few minutes, they'd move heaven and earth to meet her—and welcome Sam into the family. And if at first it was for Casey's sake, they'd love Sam before long. He knew it. They couldn't have brought him up with so much love and deny it to Sam forever.

Casey chatted to her grandparents, asking her usual multitude of questions. Brett's premonition grew stronger when Casey laughed at her grandpa, calling him a funny man and asking when she could come to visit.

Brett took the phone then. "Hi, Dad. Talk to Mum for a while. She has things she needs to tell you. I'll call you again in a few hours, okay? I love you."

He listened to his father's stumbling eloquence on Casey's adorable factor for a few minutes, then said, "Sam's made coffee, Dad. I'll call you back soon."

He disconnected the phone, dressed and left the bedroom, realising that again he hadn't asked, he'd just assumed. It was time for more than breakfast.

He hugged Casey briefly as he passed her in the living room. "I need to talk to Mummy, Case— and no listening in on us, okay?"

His stern, loving tone gained Casey's instant response. "Yes, Daddy. Can we play with my blocks after breakfast?"

"Sure, munchkin." He walked into the kitchen. "Can I help with anything, Sam?"

Sam turned and smiled, and try as he might, he could see no resistance, no shadows. "Just about done. I kept it simple, just toast and coffee and juice."

"Sounds good. Sam—" He hesitated for a moment. "I realise I took charge again, telling my parents we were a family without consulting you. You said last night there were no guarantees."

"There are now." Her eyes shining, she came to him, wrapped her arms around his waist, lifted her face and kissed him. "I love you, Brett. I wouldn't say it if I didn't mean it forever."

Filled with relief and love, he kissed her back, deep and strong. "I didn't want to take anything for granted. I've done too much of that in the past."

"Did you mean it about staying in Sydney?"

The little pang grew less every time he thought about it. "I love Melbourne, but if you and Casey have put down roots here, then I can, as well. Maybe we can buy this house—it's a great place. I can join a general medical practice. Statistics—"

She chuckled and buffed him on the chin. "You and your statistics, Glennon."

He grinned but went on mock haughtily, "Statistics show that the number of general practitioners has fallen per one hundred thousand in Australia, while surgeons of every kind have risen. It may not be what I wanted at first," he added, his eyes filled with love, "but I've had enough dreams come true. And being in a practice will allow more time to give to you and Casey."

"We need that," she said softly. "If you believed too much in dreams, I never believed at all. I was so frightened you'd go again and leave me with another shattered miracle."

"I'm here to stay, Sam." He held her close.

"Last night, seeing you with Casey, I believed you for the first time, and I decided I've been too much of a coward. It's time to take a chance. As you did for me, with your family," she added softly, looking up at him with so much love his heart flipped over.

He shook his head. "That was long overdue, Sam."

"No. I realised that last night, too." She touched his face. "You gave me encouragement and freedom to speak if I wanted to, but I was more comfortable with rejection. Then I could remain a victim and have you more to myself. I'm ashamed to admit it, but it's true." Her head fell to his chest. "For the sake of keeping you to myself, deep down I hoped for a family rift…and created years of pain for us both. I'm so sorry, Brett."

He kissed her hair. "We're done with the past, Sam. We have the rest of our lives to look forward to." He lifted his voice. "Hey, munchkin-head, get out here. Hug time!"

Within seconds, Casey flew into her parents' arms. "Wanna play blocks, Br—Daddy?"

"Br—Daddy. That's a new one," he teased her to get past the awkward moment. "Is that like Puff Daddy? Does he play blocks before breakfast?"

"I don't know Puff's Daddy. I don't even know Puff. You're silly, Daddy," she giggled.

"I am," he said solemnly, loving the sound of *Daddy* on his daughter's lips. "Listen up, Case. I want to ask you a question." He waited for her nod before he spoke. "I'd like to move in here, for us to be a family. What do you think?"

The grin spread across her little face as she punched his arm. "Silly Daddy. Of course you're gonna live with us! When am I getting a brother or sister?" she asked, moving on to what interested her.

Brett and Sam looked at each other and began laughing. He'd been so worried about Casey's reaction, and her underwhelming response was the funniest anticlimax he'd heard in a long time. "Give us time, okay, Case? Maybe in a year or so. But Mummy might want to keep working for a while?" he asked Sam.

But she shook her head, her eyes shining. "I could be pregnant now," she mouthed. Aloud she said, "I think I'll try being a stay-at-home mum for a while. A lady of leisure—"

Brett laughed and kissed her. His hyperactive Sam could never rest for long. "Yeah, I get the picture. I'll get a job in a few weeks—after a family holiday. I think one is in order for us all."

Sam's eyes glowed. "A second honeymoon," she breathed.

He grinned. "How about Fiji or the Whitsunday

Islands? I hear they have fantastic kid-friendly resorts." Seeing Casey's sudden paleness, remembering her terrified reaction last night to being away from the familiar, he added, "Maybe we can ask Serena and Kate along? We could pay for them to come as Casey's special friends."

And maybe he and Sam could snatch the odd romantic hour or two alone...

"I'm sure Serena would love it," Sam said softly. "How about we visit Melbourne first, Casey, and you can meet your nana and grandpa?"

The tide of pride and love filling Brett needed expression. *I am so proud of you...*

Sam's eyes glittered with the tears she was holding back. *For you. For Casey.*

Casey grinned, hopped off Brett's longsuffering hip and capered around the clean space between the kitchen counter and the dining table—her designated play area in the room. "Yeah! I wanna meet my nana and grandpa! I wanna go to Fiji with Kate!"

Brett watched her capering, saw Sam's joy, and the warmth filled his heart to overflowing.

Their family would never be average. There'd always be new challenges to meet, and they would always have to find different ways of exploring the freedoms and fun other families took for granted as their right. But Sam and Casey were *his* family—and they were together at last.

And that was more than enough of a miracle for him.

MILLS & BOON® PUBLISH EIGHT LARGE PRINT TITLES A MONTH. THESE ARE THE EIGHT TITLES FOR FEBRUARY 2007

———— ❦ ————

PURCHASED BY THE BILLIONAIRE
Helen Bianchin

MASTER OF PLEASURE
Penny Jordan

THE SULTAN'S VIRGIN BRIDE
Sarah Morgan

WANTED: MISTRESS AND MOTHER
Carol Marinelli

PROMISE OF A FAMILY
Jessica Steele

WANTED: OUTBACK WIFE
Ally Blake

BUSINESS ARRANGEMENT BRIDE
Jessica Hart

LONG-LOST FATHER
Melissa James

MILLS & BOON® PUBLISH EIGHT LARGE PRINT TITLES A MONTH. THESE ARE THE EIGHT TITLES FOR MARCH 2007

❦

PURCHASED FOR REVENGE
Julia James

THE PLAYBOY BOSS'S CHOSEN BRIDE
Emma Darcy

HOLLYWOOD HUSBAND, CONTRACT WIFE
Jane Porter

BEDDED BY THE DESERT KING
Susan Stephens

HER CHRISTMAS WEDDING WISH
Judy Christenberry

MARRIED UNDER THE MISTLETOE
Linda Goodnight

SNOWBOUND REUNION
Barbara McMahon

THE TYCOON'S INSTANT FAMILY
Caroline Anderson

MILLS & BOON®

Live the emotion

0207 Rom LP